REFLECTIONS BY THE KARYATIS IN THE BRITISH MUSEUM

It must be early morning again. The cleaning crews are gone and Lester, the young guard, has taken his usual post. Someone has turned on the bright overhead lights. Same routine as yesterday and the day before.

And I? Still here. Still in a place I'd rather not be. **A captive in the British Museum.**

* * * * *

So, this is why I am here! In a strange land where I don't want to be, all because of a vain English nobleman anxious to impress his new bride. And, because of his paranoid chaplain who talked him into believing that I needed to be rescued! Rescued from whom? How absurd.

For the record, **I did not ask to be rescued.**

PURVIEW: HER VIEW

EYEWITNESS TO HISTORY

by: **DENNIS MENOS**

VERGINA PRESS

PO Box 60661

Potomac, MD 20859

This is a work of fiction and its characters are fictitious. Any similarity to real persons living or dead is coincidental and not intended by the author.

Cover design by Victoria Barry. Art work by Cimon Psira.

To Charlotte and Victoria

As a reminder of their

Hellenic heritage

PURVIEW: HER VIEW

EYEWITNESS TO HISTORY

PREFACE

In 1802, while helping himself to the treasures of the Parthenon, Thomas Bruce, the Lord of Elgin, decided to add a Caryatid (Karyatis) statue to his collection. For over 2,200 years this beautiful maiden, along with her five sisters, had graced the temple on the Acropolis known as the Erechtheum. Eventually, the removed Caryatid found her way to the British Museum in London, where she serves today as one of its principal attractions.

Many years ago, during one of my travels to the United Kingdom, I made it a point of visiting the British Museum to view the Parthenon sculptures, or Elgin marbles, as they are occasionally known there. The sight of the Caryatid captivated me. I had never seen such beauty in a man-made object. "God, you are gorgeous!" I recall whispering, while fervently admiring her every detail.

That moment never left me. In the years since, I have wondered often what she could tell us, had she been able to speak. She had been witness, after all, to twenty-two centuries of Hellenic history, and to the most colossal art theft of all times.

This historical novel is the result.

I

IN THE BRITISH MUSEUM

It must be early morning again. The cleaning crews are gone and Lester, the young guard, has taken his usual post by the Temple of Nereid of Xanthos. Someone has turned on the bright overhead lights.

Same routine as yesterday, and the day before.

And I?

Still here. Still in a place I'd rather not be. A captive in the British Museum!

In an earlier era, Goddess Athena, daughter of Zeus the omnipotent, would have rushed to my help. I was the one statue in all of Hellas she favored most for I stood on hallowed ground, on the very spot where she had fought Poseidon, the god of the sea, for the honor of being the patron of the city of Athens. A fight which she won, of course.

But, sadly, Athena is no more.

I'll cherish always the gifts that she bestowed upon me, the ability to see all that surrounds me and to hear peoples' voices and laughter, and the talent to connect in thought with so many humans. Without these gifts, my years in captivity would have been unbearable.

I can already hear the hurried movement of the first visitors. Many are heading directly to my location. I am in Room 19 on the ground floor, around the corner from the Great Court. As a major attraction here, I draw the crowds.

A young man and what appears to be his lady friend are standing a few feet away from me. They are busy scrutinizing my every detail, my stance, my torso, even my broken arms. From their whispers and smiles, I gather that what they admire the most is my *peplos* and the way it folds over my body. Also, my braided hair combed back over my shoulders.

"She is so very elegant," I hear the man whisper.

"She certainly is," affirms his friend.

I enjoy these compliments. Not that I am vain. Listening to them is one of the few pleasures that I have left. What else can a statue do in a museum, especially if she hates being there?

"It is the Caryatid, madam," I hear a museum guide tell a visitor. "She came to us from the Acropolis in Athens."

Here we go again. More half-truths by the museum staff. What does he mean, "she came to us from the Acropolis in Athens?"

Yes, I came from the Acropolis but I did not ask to come. I was brought here by that Lord Elgin who also helped himself to the treasures of the Parthenon that are exhibited in the gallery next door.

I am a captive here! Kept against my will! I want to return home!

Isn't anyone out there listening?

The young woman who is working on some kind of a painting of my figure has just arrived. I am very glad. Watching her work helps my day pass. She is serious, focused, and unlike the many other artists who have worked on my physique before. Brush in hand, her tall frame slightly arched over the low easel on which her canvas rests, she works incessantly, alternating critical looks at me and at her canvas. Nothing seems to faze her, neither the hustle and bustle of the crowds, nor the occasional visitor who insists on openly critiquing her yet unfinished work. I am really fond of her, especially her shy smile whenever she makes eye contact with me. How I wish I could smile right back at her, to let her know that I really enjoy her being here.

But wait! Something must be troubling her today. She is just standing there, staring at me inquisitively, not once reaching for her brushes. It is so very unlike her.

"What's wrong, Caryatid?" I hear her suddenly whisper. "You seem so sad this morning, so down hearted! Whatever is troubling you, it is affecting your grace, your elegance, and regal beauty."

Her unexpected yet genuine concern stuns me. How does she know that I have the power to hear, see, and communicate -- powers granted to me by Athena, the long since discarded Olympian goddess of wisdom? If I reach out to her, will she be able to understand my thoughts?

I think, I will try.

"Yes, my young friend, something is troubling me this morning. I am still distressed over the event last evening, when Her Majesty the Queen formally opened the new Great Court of the museum."

Judging by her bewildered look my message has reached her. Poor thing, she is just standing there in near shock, her face white as a sheet unable to understand what happened. Was that the statue that had talked right back to her?

"The Great Court?" she whispers, her voice shivering with fear. "And why should that have bothered you? Everyone in London agrees that the Court is a spectacular structure."

"It may well be. But why was it necessary to celebrate the event by hosting a formal dinner in the very room where the Parthenon sculptures are exhibited? Eating and drinking, within a few feet of some of mankind's greatest art treasures?"

"You mean the Elgin marbles?"

"You may call them that if you wish, but to me they are the Parthenon sculptures. They were removed from the Parthenon on the Acropolis by Lord Elgin."

"I am familiar with the story, Caryatid. No need for you to elaborate."

"Please don't call me Caryatid! This is not my name. I am called Karyatis, Ka-ry-a-tis. I am one of six such statues that once stood on the temple of Erechtheum, on the Acropolis.

"It was Lord Elgin who removed me from my home, stuffed me in a box and had me shipped here. He had plans to do similarly with my sisters, but fortunately the gods interceded. I hear that they are all well and safe, back home where they belong, in a museum in Athens."

"I gather it is there that you'd rather be?"

"Yes!"

"But you are here now, Caryatid -- I am sorry, I meant to say, Karyatis. Being angry cannot change that. You might as well accept it and make the best of it."

"That's precisely what I have been doing all these years. Every morning I keep reminding myself that I should be patient."

"Please stop being gloomy then, for if you don't, I'll pack my things and return to my studio. I simply refuse to paint you looking as dejected and sad as this."

"No! Please don't go. I enjoy having you here. You are one of the few friends that I have. It gets awful lonely around here.

"By the way, young lady, what do people call you? What is your name?"

"Sophia."

"I like that name. It stands for wisdom, right?"

"Yes, wisdom."

"And, you are an artist?"

"Yes. I work out of a studio not far from here. On Bedford Square."

"I see. All right, Sophia. I'll do it. As a personal favor to you... I'll try to be my usual self again. But only, if you promise not to leave."

"I won't. I promise!"

"Good!

"Sophia? It's my turn now to ask a question. What prompted you to want to do a painting, portrait, or whatever else you are doing of me?"

"I am doing your portrait. I have always been fascinated by you, Karyatis. In art school, I recall sketching you several times, and I also have a large attractive bronze replica of you in my studio, along with one of Goddess Athena."

"You flatter me. But why? Why the fascination with me?"

"Your looks of course, your glorious physique, but to a large degree also because you have been around for such a very long time: two thousand, four hundred years to be precise. Do you realize what this means? There are very few objects in museums today that are older than you are.

"You were there when the twelve gods ruled Hellas from on top of Mount Olympus, when Alexander the Great launched his empire, when Rome, Byzantium, and later the Ottomans ruled the world. And now you are in London. It is a story beyond belief."

"It is true. I have seen a lot of history being made."

"Of course, you have. But why keep it to yourself, Karyatis? I, and many others I am sure, would love to hear recollections of the events that you have witnessed."

"So many events were not happy at all, Sophia. People were forever fighting and being cruel to each other."

"Unfortunately, they still are. It's the story of mankind.

"Still Karyatis, you were there during the Golden Age of Athens. You witnessed the rise and fall of mighty empires. Through the years, you must have seen and been in the presence of some of mankind's greatest figures."

"True."

"Tell me then about it. Tell me what you can remember."

"It is a big order, Sophia. I would not know where to start."

"Please do it, as a favor to me, please! And I, in return, promise to be good company and to work attentively on your portrait until it is all done."

"Till it is finished?"

"Yes. To the very end! "

The huge grin on Sophia's face confirms our understanding. I watch as she returns to her workstation, uncovers her canvas and gives her unfinished work a critical look. But suddenly, her face turns somber.

"How can I possibly tell this to Edward?" I hear her mumble. "Tell him, that I am carrying on a conversation with a statue, and that she's narrating her life's story to me? No way! I can't do that. He'll think for sure that I have lost it."

II

THE GOLDEN AGE

Perhaps, I should begin Sophia, with that unbelievable first day a very long time ago, when I came to the realization that I was unlike all other statues on the Acropolis; that, indeed, the gods had graced me with some very special gifts.

I know that it must sound incredible now, but suddenly on a very bright morning I discovered that I had the ability to see. Yes, see with my own eyes, just like you humans do. Suddenly, I could see all that was around me -- the beautiful temples near where I was standing, the gorgeous blue sky above, priests and priestesses offering sacrifices at a nearby sanctuary, and people moving about.

How can it be, I wondered? I, a lifeless statue made of stone being able to see? Could the thunder-bolt that had struck our temple earlier that morning be responsible for the miracle? It had arrived with such awesome force, it had shaken and frightened me. But it also had felt afterwards, as if a higher power from above had touched me. Were the gods playing tricks with me?

It was all so bizarre, Sophia. Not only was I able to see and marvel at all that surrounded me, but suddenly, I could also hear peoples' voices. I could actually hear men, women, and children speak and laugh and carry on. The whole thing was incredible!

"That Karyatis over there," I heard an elderly man call out, later that morning. "She is standing on the very spot where Goddess Athena fought Poseidon for the patronage of our city. She must be very special."

Is this who I am, I wondered. A Karyatis? What does it mean? Am I really very special?

"Come on, Karyatis, you don't expect me to believe this story, do you?" Sophia suddenly interrupted. "All of a sudden, out of the blue, you were able to see and hear the way we humans do? How could it be? It is obvious to me, that you have a gift of sorts for communicating with people, but hearing and seeing? No way!"

"It is the truth, Sophia. Believe me."

"You are able to see and hear at this very moment?"

"Yes."

"All right, then, prove it to me! What do I look like? What am I wearing?"

"Well, you are tall, slender and quite attractive. You are wearing what must be your favorite blue dress. You have worn it before, always with the same white scarf and a silver pin."

"Incredible! Unbelievable!" whispered Sophia in utter amazement.

To continue with my story then, Sophia. Soon after becoming aware of my surroundings, I began wondering about the temple that I was in. It appeared to be entirely new, and large crowds would stop by regularly to admire it. I would hear people refer to it as the Erechtheum.

I kept wondering. Why was it built? What goes on inside it? From where I was standing, I could see only a small part of the building. But I knew that it had to be very large because it had required fifteen years to complete. The war with Sparta, I would hear people say, had delayed the work.

I did not know then what "war" was, or whether "Sparta" was a person or something else. I do know now, of course.

As I looked around I realized that I was not alone. There were five other statues alongside me -- young women all, tall and proud, dressed in elegant long robes just like mine. Three stood beside me and two along the sides. They must be my sisters, I reasoned, because we all looked alike.

It did not take me long to discover that my sisters could neither see nor hear the way I did. They just stood there lifeless, totally oblivious to the true beauty that surrounded us. How sad, I thought, that they are unable to see what I am seeing, like that graceful temple nearby, with the tall elegant columns that people refer to as the Parthenon.

As the days passed, I became increasingly convinced that the hill on which my temple was standing was sacred to the people in the area. Why else would all those majestic and highly ornate structures have been built there? And why would people approach the area in such awe? It had to be a sacred place!

For awhile, I even believed that the gods lived there. I know better now.

No ordinary people resided on the Acropolis in those days. They lived on the plains below, in the city of Athens. Still, the Acropolis was forever crowded, even on days when the weather was not at its best. Invariably, after worshipping at the various temples and offering their sacrifices, many visitors would pause briefly in front of my temple to exchange their opinion of my sisters and me.

I really enjoyed their company, Sophia. Not only for the lavish compliments that they bestowed upon us, but also because I would learn much about life in the city from listening to their conversations. Discussions were as a rule amicable, with much give and take, except when the subject would turn to politics. Even a casual reference to Pericles, for instance, or to the war with Sparta, was bound to lead to a major argument with much shouting and finger pointing. At first, such political disputes frightened me because of their intensity and passion. But soon I discovered, that carrying on animated political discussions was a national trait of the people of Hellas, and one that they truly enjoyed.

"But why the anger at Pericles, Karyatis?" Sophia suddenly broke in. "I have always assumed that he was very popular with the people of Athens. Wasn't he the one who led the city to great power, and who rebuilt the temples on the Acropolis after their destruction by the Persians?"

"Yes, he was the one.

"I am impressed, young lady, you do know your history well."

"Not really. What little I know comes from my association with Edward."

"Edward? You mentioned him once before today. Who is he?"

"Edward is a close and trusted friend. He is a professor of history at the University of London. It is Edward's favorite pastime to reminisce on the lives and times of persons he admires in history. Pericles is one of them. The Athenian leader, I recall him saying repeatedly, was a true statesman whose influence is being felt to this day."

"Your friend is right. Pericles was good for Athens. It was the opinion held by most people at that time. Cleitarchus, certainly was one of his strong supporters."

"Cleitarchus?"

"Yes. He was an elderly schoolmaster who would make it a practice of bringing his class of young Athenian men to the Acropolis. Invariably, they would find places to sit on the slabs of marble near me, and I would listen while he instructed his young wards. He was learned and wise. Much of my knowledge about early Athenian history I owe to him."

I can almost see him now. He was short, with bushy white hair, and used a cane to conceal a limp when he walked. Judging by his appearance, and slow and deliberate movements, he was well past the prime of his life.

"Okay, men," he would announce in a stern voice, "we have to get started. Please find a place nearby where you can hear me, and remember to maintain at all times the decorum and respect to the gods that is expected of all Athenians on this holy site.

"Our study plan this morning," he began, as the young men dutifully gathered around him, "includes some of the proudest, but also saddest moments of Athenian history. We will begin by examining the life and times of our late leader

Pericles, his vision for our city, and the policies that he pursued to make his vision a reality. Without a clear understanding of the man and of his legacy, many of the tragic events that ensued -- the war with Sparta, the ill-fated expedition to Syracuse, our dwindling empire -- are impossible to comprehend.

"It is a challenge, I agree, but an essential one.

"For well over thirty years, Pericles was at the center of the political life of our city. In a way he still is, although a lot of time has passed since his death. Athenians to this day attribute to him every past glory and honor, but also every humiliation and shame, of which the city admittedly has had quite a few.

"It was under Pericles' leadership that Athens became the undisputed cultural center of Hellas, a city that thousands visited every year to marvel at its cultural and artistic accomplishments.

"Sculpture, drama, architecture, and philosophy flourished during his rule, with many of the world's greatest minds living and working in the city. The Parthenon's master sculptor Phidias, the historian Herodotus, and philosophers Protagoras and Anaxagoras, were not only citizens of Athens but also, Pericles' valued friends and close associates.

"To be sure, Pericles had his critics. He was chastised for placing a high priority on the rebuilding of the Acropolis, and for using for that purpose funds that technically did not belong to Athens. He was also criticized for squandering vast amounts on the temple honoring Goddess Athena, despite her failure many years earlier to prevent the Persian king Xerxes from defiling our city. Why does Pericles think, would ask his critics, that Athena will be more compassionate the next time we need her?"

"Master," I recall one of the young men interrupting Cleitarchus. "When Pericles decided to transfer to Athens the Delian League's treasury, from the island of Delos, which as we know he used later to erect the temples of the Acropolis, he cited as justification for his action the island's vulnerability to the Persian fleet. In view of his claim of an Athens at the center of military power, how could he admit to being unable to defend a small island the size of Delos?"

"Pericles had a vision of Athens as the center of Hellas, a city of prestige, wealth, and military power, capable of deterring another Persian invasion," answered Cleitarchus thoughtfully. "His every policy was designed to promote that vision.

"The man had an enormous following among the citizenry of Athens, and he still does many years after his death. Much of it can be attributed to the reforms that he helped introduce which made Athens synonymous with democracy -- a city governed by its own people. Pericles cherished that form of government and dedicated his entire life to offering it to every Athenian.

"To be sure, Periclean democracy had its limitations," Cleitarchus continued. "It did not extend to women, or to the thousands of foreigners, and slaves who resided in the city. Only males who were lucky enough to have been born Athenian, and who owned property, enjoyed its benefits. The assembly, the city's most visible democratic institution, failed its people repeatedly by enacting decisions that were unwise, if not outright senseless. The resolve to go to war against Sparta, the adoption of a "defensive strategy" for winning the war, the invasion of Syracuse, were all issues hotly debated in the assembly and decided upon by a majority vote. There was also that dreadful decision concerning Melos, whose entire male population was slaughtered and its women and children enslaved, all at the direction of our assembly.

"Still, democracy during the era of Pericles represented a tremendous improvement over the tyrannical governments that had ruled our city in earlier years."

"Master," another young man interjected, "had Pericles lived, would he have allowed this hideous war with Sparta to continue, which has ravaged Athens and deprived us of our empire?"

"Pericles was truly a wise and insightful leader," replied Cleitarchus. "He has been dead for quite some time now, and it is impossible to know what he would have done had he lived. Would he have allowed Spartan warriors to roam our countryside and burn our vineyards and olive groves? Would he have stood idly by while our neighbors and friends were being enslaved? I doubt it very much. I doubt it also that he would have allowed our pride, the Athenian fleet, to be decimated, as it unfortunately has been. I don't need to remind you men, that without the protection of our *triremes,* the grain ships from the Black Sea will be unable to reach the port of Piraeus and our city will be forced to surrender.

"Let's hope that it will not come to pass.

"But we are getting ahead of ourselves," he admitted, "let's look back briefly to the events that brought us to our current predicament.

"As you recall, our problems with Persia began when King Darius dispatched an invasion force across the Aegean, for the express purpose of extending Persian power over the Hellenic world. After landing on the coast of Attica, a short distance from Athens, the invading Persians began preparations for a march on the city. To forestall the need to do battle within the populated area of Athens, a force of Athenians under the command of general Miltiades, was dispatched to confront the invaders. The two armies met at Marathon where the cunning Miltiades, after outmaneuvering the much larger enemy force, succeeded in defeating it decisively. Beaten and demoralized the Persians withdrew to their ships, and departed Hellas.

"Not for long, however.

"Bent on revenge, Darius' son Xerxes, returned ten years later with a force so enormous as to make any thought of successfully confronting him on land utterly preposterous. Still, 300 gallant Spartans, under the legendary King Leonidas, intercepted the invaders at the pass of Thermopylae and held them there long enough for Athens and its allied cities to organize their defenses. Under the prodding of general Themistocles, the city of Athens itself was abandoned and its entire population withdrew to the neighboring island of Salamis. Athenian ingenuity and resourcefulness again carried the day. By cleverly maneuvering the Athenian fleet, Themistocles succeeded in enticing Xerxes into a sea battle in the narrows of Salamis Bay. For a second time the Persians were decisively defeated, and withdrew to Asia. Not before they had burned our city to the ground, however, including the *agora*, the temples on the Acropolis, and practically the entire residential area. Nothing survived the Persian fury, not even our most revered sanctuaries. The few works of art that were not destroyed during the rampage were shipped back to Persia.

"The city-states of Hellas would not have been able to withstand the overwhelming power that Xerxes thrust against them, had it not been for the fact that they were united in the face of the Persian threat. The lesson did not escape them. The Persian forces had hardly departed, when the Hellenic city-states in an unprecedented display of unity and good will agreed to organize a formal alliance to defend against a future Persian assault. The alliance which became known as the Delian League, after the island of Delos where its assembly met, counted at its peak nearly two hundred members from all corners of the Hellenic world, including city states from as far away as Asia Minor.

"Unfortunately, before too long, the Delian League, due primarily to the actions of our own assembly, began to change character, from a purely defensive alliance bent on protecting the Hellenic homeland against the Persians, to an instrument of Athenian power held together by the threat of force. Intent on dominating and enhancing its control over the alliance, Athens began instituting harsh unilateral measures against its allies, the most oppressive being the levying of a tribute on every member of the league. It undertook also the construction of a long wall, linking the city proper with the port of Piraeus. With the wall in place, and the Athenian fleet in control of the seas, no one could defeat it militarily or starve it into submission.

"Sparta, which together with its allies controlled most of southern Hellas, objected strenuously to both actions seeing in them a calculated plan by Athens to dominate the Hellenic world. Its fears were further intensified when Athens began forcing city-states to join the Delian League, whether they wished to do so or not. It also crushed attempts by cities to end their membership in the league. The island of Samos was one such member; it was dealt with harshly by Athens, when it revolted against the league.

"Before long, a number of incidents between friends and allies of Sparta and Athens aggravated the relations between the two power centers. When Sparta finally demanded, that Athens stop interfering in the affairs of its ally Corinth, Pericles prevailed on the assembly to refuse a compromise. With support for a war against Sparta running high in Athens, which many saw as an opportunity for adventure and profit, actual fighting could no longer be averted.

"Athens was confident that the war would end in its favor. The city was rich and had many allies on whom it could count for help. Its fleet controlled the trade routes to the Black Sea, and its land fortifications made it impregnable to a ground attack. The enemy had a well-trained army to be sure, but without a war fleet or a large number of ships to lay a siege on the city, and starve it to death, Athens had little to fear.

"At least this was the assessment of Pericles and at his suggestion, insistence would be a better characterization, a strategy was adopted by the assembly which relied heavily on Athenian naval supremacy to win the war. Abandon the countryside of Attica to the enemy, Pericles urged his fellow citizens, come into the city, and rely on our navy for supplies of grain and other necessities. Avoid battle with the Spartan infantry, even if it invades the countryside beyond our walls. The Spartans are incapable of really hurting us, and with our fleet conducting surprise attacks against their territory, they will be suing for peace before too long.

"So at Pericles' suggestion, Athenian farmers abandoned their lands and farms taking with them what few household goods they could, and marched into the city already crowded beyond description.

"It was a practical defensive strategy and at first all went as Pericles had predicted. Athens did not have sufficient land forces to invade and defeat Sparta, and Sparta did not have a fleet capable of overcoming the Athenians and starving them to death. The Athenian fleet would occasionally harass Sparta's allies on the Peloponnesian coast, and the Spartan infantry in turn would raid Attica, burning houses, fields and cutting down olive trees. It was a true stalemate until something very horrific happened".

"The plague!" volunteered one of the pupils.

"Yes," confirmed the schoolmaster.

"The disease probably originated in Egypt and was brought into the city by rats on board grain ships. Whatever its source, it hit Attica with vengeance. The population of Athens, living in overcrowded and unsanitary conditions as a result of Pericles' defensive strategy, had no chance. Preventive measures and medicines were to no avail, with the result that as many as a third of the population of the city succumbed to the disease. So did also Pericles.

"If you permit me to include a personal note at this point," Cleitarchus added sorrowfully, "both my parents, and two of my sisters, also fell victims to the illness.

"It would have been an opportune time for Athens to sue for peace. But Cleon, who succeeded Pericles in power, would not hear of it. Convinced that the Athenian army could defeat the Spartans in the field, he sent the army out to meet the enemy. Disaster followed, with the better trained Spartan forces repeatedly overwhelming the Athenians in battle. After several such embarrassing defeats, Nicias who in turn succeeded Cleon finally accepted a peace offer from Sparta. Its terms were actually quite generous, and Athens exited the war without major losses in territory or prestige.

"But soon, visions of a large empire began taking root again in the minds of Athenians. Acquiring the prosperous cities of Sicily, urged the charismatic but also unstable Alcibiades, would offer major economic gains and prestige to Athens wounded by the plague and the war against Sparta. Nicias was opposed to the suggestion but was soon overruled by the assembly, which not only voted in favor of an expedition of 200 ships and 10,000 men to invade Sicily, but also placed him in charge of the operation, along with Alcibiades and Lamachus.

"The affair turned out to be a disaster. The people of Sicily offered no welcome to the Athenians, and the three generals leading the expedition quarreled continuously over tactics to be followed in prosecuting the war. Before long, Sparta responded to Syracuse's plea for help, and Athens found itself again at war with the old enemy. Difficulties compounded when Alcibiades defected to Sparta, and Lamachus was killed in battle. Nicias, who had opposed the adventure in the first place, found himself in charge. In a dramatic battle in the port of Syracuse, the entire Athenian expeditionary force was decimated by the combined Spartan and Sicilian forces. By the time the battle ended, thousands of Athenians had perished, and its expeditionary fleet lay in shambles.

"It was a terrible mistake, a true blunder," lamented the schoolmaster, "and one from which our city has yet to recover. As a result of the debacle in Syracuse," he continued, "Spartan forces have again invaded Attica, and are violating our land and murdering our allies. Worse yet, as we speak, Sparta is busily constructing a fleet of *triremes* for the purpose of interdicting our supply routes to the Black Sea. You may be wondering who is behind this diabolic design? Persia, of course, which has agreed to finance the building of the required ships, in return for a Spartan promise not to interfere in Persia's designs on the Hellenic cities of Asia Minor.

"Sparta in effect," bemoaned Cleitarchus, "has given Persia a free hand over our brothers and sisters in Asia Minor. Can any of you conceive of a more grave act of treason?

"Treason! Outright treason," he repeated.

"Before concluding today's class, men, let me remind you that at our session tomorrow we will be configured as the Athenian assembly. Please come prepared to review and debate all major decisions which have affected the conduct of our war with Sparta, and far more important where we go from here. Was Pericles' defensive strategy the proper one for winning the war? Should we have undertaken the expedition to Syracuse? Once the decision had been made to dispatch a force to Sicily, shouldn't we have sent reinforcements when Sparta became involved?

"Let me assign to you, Hellenicus, the task of leading the debate on behalf of those favoring the continuation of the war. And you, Nichomachos, please serve as the spokesman for the opposition. Everyone please come appropriately prepared. I expect a lively and vigorous debate."

“Quite a sad story, Karyatis, especially of Persia exploiting the conflict between Athens and Sparta for its own purposes."

"It was typical of the way that Persia operated . By actively supporting the Spartan blockade of the port of Piraeus, it forced Athens into the realization that the war was lost.

“To everyone's great disappointment, however, it all happened without Goddess Athena, the city's patron and protector, making an effort to stop it. Her failure to act really stunned everyone.

"She really doesn't care what happens here," I would hear visitors to my temple bemoan. "Years ago she allowed the Persians to ravage our city and now it will be the Spartans."

"You, yourself, did not feel this way, Karyatis, did you?"

"As much as I hate to admit it now, I too entertained for a while serious misgivings about the goddess' commitment to our city. What else could I do, Sophia? Evidence of the impending doom was all around me: with women and children living in open poverty; wounded and infirm hoplites walking aimlessly the grounds of the Acropolis; and dozens of elderly begging or searching for food. But despite it all, there was no evidence of Athena or willingness on her part to help."

"I guess, in your position, I would probably have felt the same way."

"Thank you for saying so, but as I was soon to discover, the goddess held an entirely different view."

I realize that it must be very difficult for anyone to believe it, Sophia. But Goddess Athena, yes, the daughter of the omnipotent Zeus, who sat majestically on his throne on Mount Olympus, suddenly appeared before me one morning. It was a moment unlike anything that I had experienced before.

An enormous flash of light, more brilliant, more dazzling than one hundred Athenian suns preceded her appearance. The ground began to shake violently, and I could feel our temple struggling to remain upright. Nearly blinded by the sudden burst of light, and with my limbs trembling uncontrollably, I froze, feeling certain that the time of my demise had come.

Surprisingly, no one else around seemed to notice. The sacrifice of a couple of goats near the Parthenon proceeded uninterrupted, and so did work by the legion of slaves working in the vicinity of the new temple of Athena Nike. Apparently, I was the only one intended to perceive the event.

Her first words to me were filled with anger.

"I am curious, Karyatis," she asked. "What possessed you to want to listen to those who question my loyalty to the city? Why would you believe the lies spoken by angry and ignorant people? How could I, Athena, the patron goddess and protector of Athens, not care for what happens here? Don't you see that even the thought is preposterous?

"Do you realize how very painful this is to me? You are the most privileged statue in all of Hellas, the one that I gave the gift to see, hear, and reason like a human, yet you doubt my divinity?"

"I was not aware..." was all that I was able to whisper, still in a state of total awe. The thought of being in the presence of an Olympic deity, in front of Athena, the goddess of wisdom and whose influence extended to war and peace, the arts and literature, was impossible for me to fathom.

"You are a very special statue," she added, her voice rising in anger. "No other statue in all of Hellas has been graced with the gifts that I have bestowed upon you. Is it asking too much, then, to expect your loyalty in return? Not just occasional lukewarm loyalty, but genuine, unquestioned loyalty to me and my person at all times?"

I remained silent, praying that somehow her anger would subside. The gods, I had heard people say, bless and protect only those who honor them. Question their divinity or defile their temples, and you are due for a severe punishment.

I certainly had questioned her divinity.

Time to try to soothe her anger.

"Athena," I finally whispered. "It was foolish of me to act the way I did. I regret it. Truly, I do."

"That's all?" she snapped back.

"And I promise to be loyal to you, always," I added after a brief pause.

My words must have pleased her.

"That's more like it," she replied, her voice beginning to sound a bit more composed and unruffled.

Encouraged, I proceeded to ask her:

"Athena! You mentioned that I am a very special statue? Why is that so? Why have these special gifts been bestowed upon me? Why me?"

"You are standing on special ground, Karyatis. This is the very spot on which I fought the god of the sea Poseidon, for the right to be the protector of the city of Athens. At the height of our battle, Poseidon struck his trident into the ground and a salt-water spring erupted. But an olive tree sprang up, when in turn I struck the ground with my spear. The God Father Zeus, in whose presence we fought, declared me the winner and awarded the patronage of the city to me.

"You cannot see it from where you are standing but the olive tree still stands there. Years ago, a local artist carved my statue with wood taken from that tree. It was a charming piece of work but it did not look at all like me. It showed me having a human body, a face, arms, legs, and the like. It is really amusing; mortals continue to think of us gods as resembling them, and as having the same physical features that they have. This is far from the truth."

"Will I ever be able to view the tree?" I asked earnestly. "There are limits to what I can see from my fixed position. I am also curious to know, Athena, what the city below looks like and how people there live and work."

"I can allow you to wander below if this is your desire, but only if you remain true to your promise, never again to doubt my devotion and loyalty to this city. Never! Do you hear me?"

"I will Athena; I will always remain loyal to you," I whispered dutifully.

"I will always respect and honor you," I repeated.

"Your wish is granted," she responded. "Once a month, when the moon is full, you may wander into the city below completely unseen and unrecognized by anyone."

With these words she suddenly disappeared.

Needless to say, Sophia, this entire episode was nothing short of incredible. Please believe me, every bit of it is true.

The brief encounter did more than grant me the freedom to visit Athens. It helped me also understand the many mysteries surrounding my life on the Acropolis, and how people in the city related to their gods. Why for instance, they would build those elaborate temples for them, even though they knew full well that the gods did not reside in them. Temples, I finally realized, were designed as proof of peoples' respect for the gods.

"Yes, and also as a tribute to them," interrupted Sophia, "which explains, Karyatis, why all of Hellas was so abundantly adorned with temples during the years that you lived on the Acropolis. You were familiar, of course, only with those in Athens, but temples honoring Goddess Athena could be found in many other cities. In Corinth, Aegina, and Thebes, for instance, were temples that were renowned for their great beauty. Elaborate temples honored also Demetra and Dionysos. She was being venerated because of her power over the annual grain harvest, and he because he saw to it that there would always be an abundance of wine for the masses to enjoy.

"As an artist and lover of Hellenic art, Karyatis, I spent untold hours studying and analyzing the major temples of Hellas, their architecture and décor. In the case of the Parthenon especially, it is an enormous thrill for me, believe me, to be in touch with someone who had the opportunity to admire the temple first hand, before wars, earthquakes, religious fanaticism, and plunder marred it permanently."

"Thank you for the kind words, Sophia, The process of damaging the Parthenon began with the early Christians, and continued later by peoples of other faiths. I lived through it all, observing in anguish as our exquisite temple dedicated to Goddess Athena became first a church to a new religion, then a mosque, and finally to be nearly demolished by that madman Morossini. I'll have to tell you more about him later."

"Were you able to witness these events from where you were standing?"

"Not always. Because of the orientation of my temple I had only a partial view of the Parthenon, and it was at some distance."

"Could you make out the statue of the goddess herself, inside the temple?"

"Oh, yes! There was no way that one could miss it. Even from a distance, Athena looked dazzling! Stunning, radiant, would perhaps be better descriptions."

"The same could be said, I gather, for the decor of the temple itself. Most art critics consider the Parthenon's frieze, its metopes and pediments to have been more beautiful than the monument itself."

"Art critics, Sophia? Why would you need art critics for that? Much of the décor of the Parthenon is right here in this building, next door, remember? Do I need to remind you again of Lord Elgin?"

"You sound angry."

" Shouldn't I be?"

"I am sorry. I did not mean to reopen old wounds."

"Apology accepted."

"Fine! Now tell me, Karyatis. With only a partial view of the Parthenon how did you acquire the intimate knowledge of the temple which you obviously possess?"

"I learned a great deal from listening to Dimitrios, the local sage, Sophia. He would lead visitors on tours of the Acropolis. Whenever I would see him walking up the Propylaea in the company of others, I knew I would be in for a special treat."

Dimitrios looked always tired, head and shoulders bent, and was dressed in a gray robe over an old and soiled *chlamys.*

I can still recall the day that I first took notice of him. It was about the time that the war with Sparta was coming to an end. He had come walking up the hill, in the company of a dozen men. Judging from their attire and dialect, I knew that they could not be Athenian. I discovered later that they were visitors from the allied city of Decelea. I strained to catch a glimpse of them as they came by. They were young men, but had the overall demeanor of mature grown persons. Their stride was slow, at times weary, which was hardly surprising. Everyone was dejected in those days. The Spartan navy was patrolling the Aegean, and food in the city was in short supply. Defeat in the hands of Sparta was only a matter of time.

"Esteemed citizens of Decelea," I recall him proclaim that morning. "Before all else, let me extend to you a warm welcome to our city, our Acropolis, and to the temple of Goddess Athena. You are true and loyal friends who have stood by us through some of the harshest years of the war, and for this we are most grateful.

"This is a first visit on the sacred hill for many of you, so perhaps, a brief introduction might be in order.

"Our late leader Pericles had a grand vision, for Athens to become the center, not only of Hellas, but of the entire civilized world. The magnificent temples all around you are part of that vision.

"It was indeed a glorious day for Athens when the temple to Goddess Athena that we will be visiting, was inaugurated.

The event coincided with the goddess' birthday, and as you can well imagine, the entire area from the *agora* to the Acropolis was overflowing with humanity. There were guests from every city and village of Hellas; even from Sparta. The Erechtheum, before which we are now standing, and the Temple of Athena Nike had not been built then, but most of the Propylaea were in place. Pericles, whose purpose in rebuilding the Acropolis was to honor the gods for their help in the wars against the Persians, was present and so were all his closest friends. Herodotus, Phidias, Protagoras, Anaxagoras, all the leading thinkers and artists of the day were here.

"The Parthenon was intended as the supreme architectural achievement of the "new Athens." That it turned out as grandiose and awe-inspiring as it did, was due primarily to the efforts of three persons: the architects Kallikrates and Iktinos, who did the basic design work, and the artistic genius of Phidias, who led all its sculptural decorations. Pericles himself had picked the three men for the work, and spent enormous amounts of time with them reviewing their plans and debating every aspect of the temple's design and construction.

"The Parthenon, being dedicated to the Goddess Athena, includes a gigantic statue of her in gold and ivory. It stands inside the *cella,* or inner temple, and although only priests and priestesses are allowed there, once we approach the monument you will be able to gain a glimpse of the statue . Athena is shown standing and armed in her role as the defender of Athens. Her facial expression is calm and thoughtful, characteristic of her wisdom and purity. In her right hand she is holding a winged figure of Nike (the goddess of victory), and with her left, a spear. The statue is known Athena Parthenos, not to be confused however with Athena Promachos, the colossal and highly decorated bronze statue that you admired earlier on entering the Acropolis. Incidentally, those of you who have served at sea must know, that ships destined for Athens, often utilize the statue of Athena Promachos as a guide into the harbor of Piraeus, by following the sparks which are produced when sunlight strikes the bronze of the statue. Both, Athena Parthenos and Athena Promachos, were carved by Phidias.

"The Parthenon is actually the second such temple to grace this site on the Acropolis. The earlier structure was destroyed by the Persians, when they occupied our city briefly after the battle of Thermopylae and laid all Athens in ashes. I can still recall the pain in my father's voice whenever he would recollect this event. As a young man, he stood on the shore of the island of Aegina across the bay, where he and his family had fled because of the invading Persians, and watched in horror as the flames of the burning Acropolis turned red the Athenian sky.

"Construction of the Parthenon and of its sculptural decorations," Dimitrios continued, "required fifteen years. Marble from the nearby mountain of Penteli was used exclusively. This marble, perhaps some of you have already noticed it, despite its brilliant white color has the characteristic of appearing a soft yellow under certain light conditions.

"Separating the marble from its source in Penteli, and transporting it to the construction site, was in itself an enormous undertaking. Every summer when the roads would be dry and hard, the loads of marble coming from the quarry were a regular occurrence. People would leave their life's chores and cares, to gaze at the spectacle of the enormous mule-drawn vehicles slowly making their way through the maze of the city streets and then up the hill to the Acropolis.

"The temple itself, as you can observe, is rectangular in shape with eight Doric columns at its narrow east and west sides, and seventeen columns each along its two long sides. Doric columns surround also the wall of the *cella,* or inner temple, where the statue of Athena Parthenos is housed as well as at its east and west entrances.

"In designing the Parthenon, to forestall the building from giving the appearance of a rectangular box, Kallikrates and Iktinos introduced numerous architectural refinements. Thus, although the building itself is symmetrical throughout and its major components are in precise proportion to each other, its columns are narrowed and slightly tilted inward toward the top to create a visual illusion pleasant to the eye. Hundreds of masons, sculptors, smiths, and stone cutters worked on the project.

"The temple's sculptural decorations consist entirely of Doric art, except for the frieze on the walls of the *cella,* which is adorned with Ionic art. All surfaces have some form of sculptural decoration, even though at times this may not be fully visible to the casual observer.

"The metopes -- the rectangular slabs above the architrave, of which there are ninety-two, depict scenes from early mythology. On the west side of the temple, former residents of our city are battling the Amazons, while on the east, gods and giants are engaged in mortal struggle which the gods of course have won. The metopes on the north side of the temple display scenes from the sack of Troy (a triumphal moment in

Hellenic history), while on the south are highlights of the battle between Centaurs and Lapiths. The Centaurs, as you recall, had been invited to the wedding feast of the king of the Lapiths, and after becoming drunk attempted to carry off the Lapith women. The metopes depict Centaurs and Lapiths locked in battle for the right to the women.

"In contrast to the metopes that generally depict battles between the forces of order and justice on one hand and those of evil on the other, the Ionian relief frieze along the exterior walls of the *cella* depicts scenes from everyday life. The event depicted is that of the procession to the Panathenaea Festival, which as most of you are aware, is celebrated every four years on the birthday of the Goddess Athena. Two processions are depicted on the frieze, both beginning at the southwest corner and ending on the east side. One moves along the west end and north side, the other along the south side. At the eastern end of the cella, Goddess Athena in the presence of Zeus and other gods is presented with a *peplos* woven by the maidens of Athens. This enormous sculpture, along the frieze, includes hundreds of human figures and animals in a great variety of activities, with the gods at the east end observing the procession.

"With the Parthenon being dedicated to Goddess Athena, it is only natural that scenes from her life would be amply depicted. At the pediment above the main entrance on the east side, are scenes from her birth. Zeus is standing at the center, with Athena and Hephaistos next to him. It was Hephaistos who opened the head of Zeus with an axe so that the goddess could be born. Sitting nearby are other deities, including Hera, Poseidon, Hermes, Ares, Apollo, and Artemis. The west pediment depicts the fight between Athena and the god of the sea Poseidon, for the right to be the patron deity of the city of Athens. Athena emerged victorious from this fight, and has remained since our champion and the one we trust to guard our city."

At this point, Dimitrios would come to the end of his prepared remarks. "Please, friends, feel free to look around," he would urge the visitors. "You may wish to visit also our newest temples, the Erechtheum not quite completed yet and also the one honoring Athena Nike. The Erechtheum, owes its name to Erechtheus who was a local hero and legendary king of our city. It is very unlike other temples in Hellas, in that it includes a portico whose roof is held up by six maidens, instead of the customary columns. The maidens are depicted in a tranquil stance, each slightly different from her sisters."

"Little did Dimitrios know, Sophia, that one of these maiden -- I of course -- would eventually end up here in this museum".

"A wooden statue of Athena," Dimitrios would continue, "is housed in the *cella* of the Erechtheum. Though less magnificent than Phidias' gold and ivory statue in the Parthenon, the Erechtheum statue is a lot older and considered more sacred.

"Before leaving, let me wish you all Godspeed and a safe return home. I would like also to extend a cordial invitation to everyone to our city's next Panathenaea Festival. The gods willing, it will be held again when this tragic war with Sparta is ended. The entire city honors Goddess Athena at these Festivals with a march up the Acropolis, followed by the presentation to her of the *peplos*. The festival concludes with a banquet in which thousands participate, amid lavish musical and theatrical entertainment and athletic competitions. I look forward to seeing you all here. Please make every effort to attend."

"I am astounded, Karyatis, at your ability to recall events of so long ago. Also, at your extraordinary ability to communicate with others as you have been doing with me."

"They were gifts from the goddess, Sophia. For a long time, however, I hesitated using them. Even after my first contact with humans which occurred with an Athenian woman, it took a lot of getting used to. Me, a simple statue communicating with real living human beings, and having my messages received by them and responded to? It was bizarre and frightening at first."

It all began when a tall slender woman, obviously an Athenian, approached my temple on a balmy fall afternoon. She was unlike the many visitors who regularly stopped by to admire my sisters and me. She came alone, walking slowly, almost deliberately, and judging by the sadness on her face she was in great anguish.

For a while she just stood there motionless looking directly at me, as if uncertain of what to do next.

"Oh how I wish, Karyatis," I heard her whisper suddenly, "that I had never been born an Athenian. I simply can no longer endure the human suffering that surrounds me, this dreadful war with Sparta which our city can never win, the famine and the shameful treatment of women in defeat."

She was actually addressing me. I could see it in her eyes. She was imploring me to listen.

"Why did fate dictate that I be born an Athenian?" she continued. "To merely serve as a sacrificial animal in an insane war? To surrender to that madness everything and everyone that I hold dear? My only son, barely a grown man, drowned near Cape Sounion last month when his *trireme* fell victim to a deceitful attack by the Spartan navy. His demise followed that of his father, who five years earlier had sacrificed his life on the ramparts of the Long Wall.

"Forgive me if I sound irate," she added, " but I am returning from a performance of *Trojan Women* in the Theater of Dionysos, by our great playwright Euripides. I should never have gone for the play left me totally unnerved. *The Women,* I am sure you don't know it, deals with the story of the mothers, widows, and children of Troy in the aftermath of the conquest of their city by warriors from Hellas.

"It was truly heartbreaking to listen to Queen Hecuba of Troy surveying the smoking ruins of her once glorious city, and to bemoan the death of her husband Priam, the ravaging of her daughter Cassandra, and the killing of her six- year old grandson Astyanax, thrown to his death from the city walls by the victors of the war. It made no difference that she was the queen of the enemy city. She was a wife, and a mother first, like myself.

"Euripides conceived the play, they say, to depict the dreadfulness of war and the high price that women and children must pay in its aftermath. But you know what Karyatis? I think, he also had another motive. He wanted to censure Athens for its senseless sacking not long ago of Melos, an ally of Sparta. The entire city was razed to the ground by our forces, and its every building and structure turned to dust and rubble. As for the men of Melos? They were executed in a senseless display of cruelty, while their women and children were sent to exile. How cruel! How very shameful!"

I listened in amazement, unable to perceive how Athenian men, the same ones who regularly visited here to offer sacrifice to the gods, were capable of inflicting such pain on fellow human beings. Was the kind of cruelty administered upon the women and children of Melos, typical of warfare in Hellas, I wondered? Why should innocent persons become victims of a war, that they themselves had not been instrumental in initiating?

Melos must have been an exception, I surmised.

"No, Karyatis, Melos was not an exception," she answered, forcefully. "Treating an enemy in such cruel manner is not unheard of in Hellas. It is precisely what happened also to the city of Scione, when Athenian forces after reducing it by siege proceeded to kill all its adult males, enslave its women and children, and give the land which the city formerly occupied to the Plataeans to live on.

"Surprised? Don't be! The same fate almost met the island city of Mytilene, when it attempted to revolt against Athens. Even though it had surrendered and accepted as punishment the stationing of an Athenian garrison on its territory, the Athenian assembly -- our own fellow citizens -- voted to have its entire male population killed, and its women and children sold into slavery. A *trireme* with orders to carry out the sentence was sent to the island. Fortunately, the following morning, the assembly had second thoughts and another *trireme* was dispatched to the island to countermand the earlier order. It arrived, just on time, to prevent the death of thousands of innocent people.

"Do you understand now," she asked in a rising voice, "do you see why I am frozen with fear? The war with Sparta is all but lost and I, my family and friends, could suffer the same fate in the hands of the Spartan victors, as the women and children of Troy did, and of Melos and Scione. too.

"And don't think for a moment , Karyatis, that life in Hellas for us women is much better in peacetime. I hope you don't take all the talk of us being citizens of Athens seriously. Yes, we are citizens, but only because we give birth to Athenian males. We are not allowed to inherit or own property, are not permitted to run for public office, or to participate in the workings of our city. We are not even allowed to attend the sessions of the assembly. When we are called to appear before a court, we must bring along a male legal guardian to speak for us. Politics and the exercise of democracy are male prerogatives in democratic Athens!"

"Is this why so relatively few women venture out on the streets in daytime?" I wondered.

"Of course! A woman in Athens, Karyatis, is not allowed out of her home except for proper reason, such as to attend a religious festival, a funeral, or to assist in the childbirth at the home of a relative or friend. Our days are devoted exclusively to working around the house, and to caring for our husbands and children. We are expected to be good housekeepers, discreet, and to manage the affairs of our household. But even in our own homes we are limited as to what we can do. We are not allowed, for instance, into the rooms occupied by the men and must perform all our chores in interior rooms. Let's face it, we are second class-citizens, not much better than slaves."

"There must be exceptions, aren't there?" I asked."You, yourself, attended a theater performance earlier today. Also what about Aspasia, Pericles' much beloved mistress. She certainly was not a slave!"

"Of course not. But Aspasia was not an Athenian. She was born and raised in Miletos, a settlement on the western coast of Asia Minor. As a foreigner, she was not bound by the same laws and customs that confine us to our households.

"Then too, she was a woman of great beauty and intelligence, one must admit that, with a singular ability to attract the company of powerful and learned men. She was of course Pericles' mistress, but reportedly Socrates, Plato, and many other philosophers and artists of the day also enjoyed her company. Plato, in fact, referred to her as his teacher in the theory of love. She enjoyed a life of constant stimulation and excitement, and kept her home open at all times to anyone willing to debate her on matters of philosophy, literature and the arts.

"Pericles and Aspasia were devoted to each other and she proved herself his worthy partner, both in his political ambitions and his desire to adorn Athens with great works of art. Against all laws and customs, which required that women in Athens be unseen and unheard, Pericles consulted her openly and showed much affection to her in public.

"Athens never forgave her, however, for causing the breakup of Pericles' marriage. She was accused of being a prostitute, and a procurer of women for her husband and his friends. But Pericles stood by her. When later she was accused also of atheism, he appeared in court with her and defended her in tears."

My visitor suddenly fell quiet. The appearance of an elderly couple nearby made continuation of our encounter inappropriate. I watched, as she slowly began the trek down the hill. She looked a lot more composed and calm than when she first came. Opening her heart to me must have helped!

"What happened to Aspasia after Pericles died?" I wondered. "Did the city finally forgive her? Has she found a new partner in life?"

"Not now, Karyatis," she whispered. "Some other time, perhaps."

"I hope you come back," I added. "There are dozens of questions that I would like to ask you."

"What a sad story, Karyatis. Did you ever see the woman again? Did she return?"

"She did, Sophia, when the war with Sparta ended."

"The war is finally over," she announced in a matter of fact tone one afternoon.

"Sparta will rule supreme from this day on." There was sadness in her voice as she spoke, but no anguish or agony of the kind that she had displayed during her first visit.

"Famine has finally brought Athens to its knees, Karyatis. Led by Lysander, the Spartan navy has succeeded in destroying the few remaining Athenian *triremes,* and with our ships gone, any hope of bringing grain to our starving people and continuing the struggle has ended. Lysander's terms understandably are harsh, but fortunately, do not call for razing our city or killing its men and enslaving its women and children.

"There will be no repeat of the massacres of Troy or Melos, no slaughter of innocent women and children, even though according to rumors in the agora, Sparta's ally Corinth is demanding that the Athenian practice of killing all enemy men and the selling of women and children into slavery, be applied also to the defeated Athenians.

"But Sparta has prevailed, and there will be no massacre. It is demanding however, that we destroy all our remaining *triremes*, dismantle our fortifications, and also take down the wall that connects the port of Piraeus with our city. It has also directed that we do away with our democratic form of government and accept as our future leaders thirty pro-Spartan tyrants."

"All and all not a bad deal, don't you agree?" I inquired.

"Yes, one with Athena's imprint on it!"

"At the end, Goddess Athena did protect the city and saved it from catastrophe," interrupted Sophia, "just like she was supposed to."

"Yes. And she also made sure that the Spartan rule would not last. Before long, Thebes became the new power center in Hellas, and in two battles demolished the myth of Spartan military invincibility. The supremacy of Thebes, however, was similarly short-lived. A new power, under the Macedonian King Philip and its legendary son Alexander, was slowly making its presence felt."

"Oh, yes. I want to hear your recollections on both these men. Tomorrow, perhaps, Karyatis?"

"Certainly!"

"But first, may I ask you? Did you ever venture into the city, all alone, as she said you could?"

"I did; but it sure was a scary experience at first."

Ever since Goddess Athena had said that I could, I had this uncontrollable desire, Sophia, to wander into the city below and observe with my own eyes how people lived and worked.

From where I was standing, I could barely make out the city of course. I could see houses and people, but not much else. Most homes were modest in size and were wedged tightly against each other along narrow winding streets. A few, probably those belonging to wealthier Athenians, were larger and included what appeared to be several rooms enclosing a courtyard. I would often wonder what life was like inside these homes. Were women really no better off than slaves, as the Athenian woman had complained to me earlier?

There was little doubt in my mind, of course, that men in Athens led a privileged life of sports, leisure and politics. Except during the times they went to war, I hardly ever saw them working. But, not so, when it came to foreigners and slaves. They were constantly on the go, carrying materials to building sites, helping with the construction of buildings, and transporting water from local fountains and springs to the homes of the more affluent. I kept wondering. How did these people ever become slaves?

I know now, of course. They were the lucky ones who had survived a war and its aftermath.

As for my first visit to the agora? It happened on a beautiful evening when Athens was literally aglow by a moon, brilliant beyond belief. Could this be the time that she had prescribed as the moment for my freedom, I wondered?

Feelings of extreme anxiety suddenly engulfed me. If I venture into the city below, I began thinking, how will I ever find my way through the maze of monuments and people? More important, will I be able to return safely home and rejoin my sisters?

For a brief moment, I even considered giving up the entire idea.

"Don't be such a coward, Karyatis," I heard suddenly the unmistakable voice thundering from above. I didn't even have to look up. It had to be her.

As intense energy began surrounding me, as her dazzling, brilliant figure suddenly appeared in front of me. But as in the case of her earlier appearance, only I was aware of her presence.

"Why do you hesitate going into the city?" she asked kind of annoyed. "Didn't I explain to you, that no one will ever know of you being there? It is part of you being "very special," remember?"

Her appearance at the precise moment that I was having second thoughts about the entire venture made me shudder. Is she aware of my every thought, I wondered? Even of the moments when my belief in her falters?

"Come on! Let's go," she commanded, "I'll show you the way."

I followed her obediently.

"This Karyatis is the Theater of Dionysos, probably the most famous and popular of all Athenian institutions. Because of its location on the foothills of the Acropolis, below the Parthenon, you cannot see it from your normal position. But you must have known of its existence from the roar of the crowds which greets the plays of Sophocles, Aeschylus, and Euripides whenever they are performed here.

"It is enormous, isn't? There were four thousand Athenians gathered here this afternoon, for a performance of *Oedipus Rex*.

"Across from the theater, on the other side of the divide," she continued, "are two extremely important sites: the Pnyx, where Athenians meet to debate the affairs of their city, and the hill of Arios Pagos, home of the city's highest court. Of the two, the Pnyx is by far the liveliest, especially during elections when the *strategi* or leaders for the year, are selected by the people. In the Arios Pagos are heard only cases of murder and treason. Some of the most sensational trials in the city's history have been tried here, including not long ago the trial of Alcibiades, who shamelessly betrayed Athens during its expedition to Syracuse."

She paused. "See? It's not so bad is it?" she asked in a tone clearly designed to encourage me to go it alone from this point on. " No one is aware of us being here."

I remained silent, still not being up to it.

"And this of course is the *agora*," she continued," the political, cultural and business center of the city. It is always jammed, always busy, very much like it is this evening. The *agor*a serves as the meeting place for politicians, artisans, and peasants, and is the place to meet friends, to be seen and conduct business. Farmers bring their produce here to sell directly to the public, and so do tradesmen and artisans of all kinds."

"So many buildings! So many people! It is an awesome sight," I managed to whisper.

"That it is, but keep in mind Karyatis, that we are standing at the very spot where all significant commercial activity of the city is transacted, and all major decisions affecting its future are made. Most Athenian administrative buildings, courts, temples and shrines are located here.

"Over there, for instance, squarely in the center of the *agora,* is the Altar of the Twelve Gods, one of the city's most sacred sites. It is dedicated to me, to my father Zeus, and to several other Olympian gods and goddesses. Its sanctuary has been used in the past as a refuge. Anyone seeking shelter here during the night when the moon is full is free of prosecution until the next full moon.

"The large narrow buildings on both sides of the *agora,*" she continued, "the ones with the open colonnades are known as *stoas.* It is here, and in the small nearby private shops and stalls, that Athenians come to make their purchases of meat, vegetables and fruit. Custom dictates, however, that slaves, rather than the women of the household buy the provisions. But the *stoas* are also favorite venues for Athenians to congregate, debate politics and argue over the affairs of their city.

"There is an old saying in Athens, that if you are looking for someone, you will most likely find him at the Voulefterion. That's the elegant building not far from here, the one surrounded by the statues of the twelve Olympian gods. Five hundred Athenian men elected to this office meet here daily to provide continuity in the administration of the city between sessions of the assembly. The debate in the Voulefterion is always animated and full of surprises, which explains the large number of citizens who trek daily to the building. Next door is the Stratigion, home of the ten *strategi* who rule Athens. The pace of activity here is a lot more subdued; still, each *strategos* likes to meet with many of the citizens that he represents, which explains the large crowds that are always seen milling around the building.

"Have you had enough of Athens for a while?" she wondered.

I sensed that she was anxious to leave.

"Yes," I replied, "but would love to return again on another day."

"You'll have to do it on your own next time, Karyatis. Make sure that you also visit that elegant Doric temple near the hill of Arios Pagos, the one that people refer to as the Hephaistion. It is the largest religious shrine in the *agora*."

"Was it built to honor Hephaistos?"

"Don't let the name deceive you. The temple is actually dedicated to me, as well as to Hephaistos. If you look carefully, between the columns at the north end of the temple, you'll notice a bronze statue of me. It does not look at all like me, but presumably this is what I look like in the mind of its artist. The thought must have amused her, because I could hear her chuckle.

"Karyatis, you are in for a treat," she called out as she was leaving. "The elderly man with the bushy white hair, the one who is addressing the crowd in front of the *stoa* is Socrates, one of the most influential figures of the city, and also its most controversial. I hope you'll get a chance to hear him speak, sometime."

They were her last words.

"Well, did you, did you ever get a chance to listen to him speak?" Sophia asked eagerly. She had stopped all work on her painting, being totally engrossed in the Karyatis' story.

"No, I never did. In the weeks that followed, Socrates was charged, tried and sentenced to death for insulting the gods, and corrupting the youth of Athens."

"I recall Edward mentioning once that Socrates' trial and sentencing were spurious affairs, designed to uplift Athens after its disastrous war with Sparta."

"Probably true, Sophia. Socrates was enormously popular in the city. But unfortunately, he had also many bitter enemies. The slanders and lies of his foes finally did him in."

"Could we start tomorrow's session with your recollections of his life? Please don't forget also Edward's two favorites, Philip of Macedonia and his son Alexander."

"They were my favorites, too. Incidentally, will you be seeing Edward this evening?"

"No, he is still in Washington. He has been there for nearly three months, researching Byzantine coins at Dumbarton Oaks."

"Coins? I am not sure that I understand."

"I'll have to explain it all some other time. I must run now. It's my evening with the Girl Guides and I don't want to be late. The Guides are my favorite organization. I spent many years with them as a young girl, and made several lifelong friendships. Helping my troop now is my way of giving back for all the gifts I received. It is also helping me keep in touch with today's generation of young Britons."

"Will you get a chance to speak to Edward this evening?"

"Probably."

"When you do, will you please give him my regards?"

For a minute, Sophia just stood there, as if searching for a proper reply.

"You must be kidding, Karyatis." she responded in exasperation. "You really expect me to tell the man that I love, that a statue that I have been conversing with is sending him regards? If I do, he'll surely think that I need immediate medical attention."

"I understand."

"Good bye then, and please stay out of trouble while I am gone."

"Now you are being funny, Sophia! Get into trouble staring at three museum walls and an Ionic column all night long?"

"At least, the column is made of the same Pentelic marble, as you are."

"Yes. And it also came from the same temple, the Erechtheum, as I was. Unfortunately we both caught Elgin's eye."

III

INTERLUDE

On route to her Girl Guide troop, after a strange but also stimulating five hours in the British Museum where she had "connected" with a statue, a supernatural act to be sure but one that she was absolutely certain had occurred, Sophia found herself deep in thoughts. It had not been the recollections of the Caryatid on the times and deeds of Pericles that had brought her suddenly to that state of mind. Despite her generally limited knowledge of world history, she had been aware of the basic facts surrounding classical Athens -- its struggle to prevail over the other city-states, and its disastrous war with Sparta. Edward often enjoyed talking to her about that period, and she remembered hearing highlights of Caryatid's own story from Dr. Sarah Jones, her professor of art history at the University of Leeds.

Sophia's thoughts that evening were clearly the result of Caryatid's remark as she was preparing to leave. "Will you be speaking with Edward this evening?" she had asked, "when you do, please give him my regards." The comment, normal for a statue was totally eerie to a human mind.

"You must be kidding," she recalled responding to her in exasperation. "How can I possibly tell the man that I love, that I have been conversing with a statue," or words to that effect? "If I did, he'll think for sure that am in need of immediate medical attention."

But the more that Sophia considered Caryatid's comment, the more weird it really became. Sooner or later she would have to let Edward in on her little secret. How would he react to this clearly inexplicable episode, and to her sudden curiosity in history, a subject that she had told him repeatedly that it was beyond her life's main interests? Worse yet, how would he, a trustee of the British Museum, react to her probing on one of the museum's most prized possessions; how it happened to be in London, or whether it should continue to remain there?

In the four years that she had known Edward, there had not been many secrets between them. She had even told him of her biggest secret yet, the one that she had held back from nearly everyone else for fear of being ridiculed, of her belief in reincarnation and of her many visits to a therapist in Bath in search of clues to her prior life. Edward was stunned by her admission when she first broached the subject, and tried in vain to convince her otherwise. Most people in the world, she reminded him emphatically, are convinced that they have lived before or that they will be reborn on this earth, and I am one of them. The entire subject sounded so uncanny to him that after several futile attempts at an accommodation, they agreed to disagree by not discussing it again. And they never did, except once, when out of the blue Edward asked Sophia: "If you think that you have lived before on this earth, who do you believe you were?" Without the least of hesitation Sophia replied: " I am sure that I was there, Edward, on the Acropolis in Athens, at some point. I don't know precisely when or in what capacity, but I was there. Perhaps, as the wife of someone important, or a priestess in the service of Goddess Athena, or even a maiden of sorts in the court of a semi-goddess. There is not the slightest doubt of that in my mind, Edward." During the summer that followed her admission, Edward was left cooling his heels in London, while Sophia in Athens was exploring every conceivable archaeological site within the city for clues of her prior life.

Until the day she had ventured her first words to the Caryatid, only to be shocked by receiving her totally unexpected response, Sophia had only a mild interest in the world of history. Art history, yes; the accomplishments of the great masters, yes; but descriptions of empires long gone, alliances, kings ,and wars, no way. They held little interest to her.

Suddenly however, she was feeling a rising curiosity about the history of the land where once she might have lived. The Caryatid had hit only the highlights in her brief vignettes, focusing on the events that she was able to observe or learn about from listening to peoples' conversations. But there was so much more that she had failed to cover. Would one of Caryatid's stories possibly throw light into her own past?

Her phone was ringing stubbornly, as she opened the front door of her studio.

"Good evening, Edward," she answered, knowing full well who the person would be at the other end of the line. "The streets were mobbed with Christmas shoppers this evening, so I took my time walking back from the Guides."

It was a fib and she knew it. Since leaving the museum and even while illustrating for her young Guides the best technique for mixing colors, she had found herself in such deep thoughts, she had barely noticed the Christmas crowds.

It was midnight in London when Edward concluded his phone call to Sophia. As was their practice, they exchanged news of the day, messages from friends, and invitations to events of interest to one or both of them. She had been working faithfully, she said, on her portrait of the Caryatid, and also struggling with bitter cold weather and a landlady who refused to repair a leaky window in her studio. Edward, in turn, reported spending his morning between doing paper work in his tiny Georgetown apartment, and research at the Dumbarton Oaks Library.

"The Dumbarton mansion, Sophia, with its acres of formal gardens and great oak trees," he remarked, "is one of the most beautiful spots in town. How I wish, it was springtime and you were here to enjoy it all with me."

"I visited there briefly, Edward, as you remember, during my junior year at American University. My recollection is of an extremely beautiful and very busy place. But, Edward," she continued, "what are you doing day dreaming? It will be another three months before spring arrives."

"I guess, these cold dreary days in Washington are getting to me."

"Oh, Edward!" she replied, in a manner clearly designed to indicate compassion.

"I've got some good news," she continued. "I stopped by your flat. Your mail has been picked up and is stacked up on the hallway table, your plants have been watered, and the refrigerator has been cleaned. I assume Nelly did it all out after you left. Really, Edward, you don't pay her enough. She cleans after you better than any housekeeper I know. Anyway, you have three invitations for benefits in the spring waiting for you."

"Thanks for looking into it. And how was your meeting with the Guides?"

"Fun as usual. I showed the girls how to mix colors (some made a huge mess on their uniforms), and then I surprised each with a new badge, a prize from me for learning about the flowers of England. The girls promised to do sketches of these flowers and include them in their Christmas Day greetings to their Mothers. "

"As I've said so many times before, Sophia. The girls are lucky to have you!"

"You are always saying the nicest things, Edward. And how is your project coming along? It is getting close to Christmas, you know."

"Yes, and also the beginning of the next semester."

"Will you be carrying your usual load when you return? In both positions?"

"Yes, but I must finish first what I have started here. There are still dozens of coins that I have to go through. They are actually only a small fraction of the Byzantine coin collection at Dumbarton Oaks. As you know, I am focusing only on those in use during the Komninos dynasty."

Sophia's reference to "both positions" were to the posts that Edward held at London University, as the administrator of the Department of History and of the Institute of Historical Research. The two positions kept him totally preoccupied and it was not until he had completed ten years of service, along with several awards for superior scholarship, that he was finally granted a temporary leave of absence, which led to his three-month fellowship at Dumbarton Oaks.

As much as Edward had been looking forward to examining firsthand his beloved Byzantine coins, leaving Sophia behind for such an extended period concerned him greatly. There was E-Mail, of course, and low cost transatlantic phone calls, and Skype to keep in touch. But he was aware of her inclination to spend evenings alone, as well as of her penchant for working around-the-clock at the start of any new project, such as the portrait of the Caryatid. She was almost a masochist in that regard.

Sophia had relatively few friends and practically no family, having been raised by an aunt, after a tragic fire very early in her life had deprived her of both her parents. While at the university she had gotten emotionally involved with one of her professors, a married man at that, who took great pleasure in fracturing her heart. Deeply hurt, and slow to recover, Sophia sought healing by keeping to herself and immersing in her art. It was then, that Edward entered her life.

They met on the very day that he had been appointed to succeed his late father as a trustee of the British Museum, an enormous honor for someone from academia with only average family connections, and a limited track record for fund raising. Their first date, dinner at an elegant Russian restaurant in Mayfair, had hardly been a rousing success. Edward did most of the talking on his favorite subject -- historical heroes that he admired most; that evening it was Peter the Great of Russia -- while Sophia listened. Six months later, after becoming fully convinced that Edward was totally unlike her earlier lover, and the right man for her, Sophia agreed to seeing him exclusively, spending most evenings and weekends together attending concerts and visiting galleries with artists from the London arts colony. But despite their increasing closeness and obvious love, an overcautious Sophia never allowed the subject of marriage to come up.

IV

MACEDONIA PREVAILS

I hear that London was blanketed by a huge snow storm during the night. Streets are slippery and schools are closed. Only a few visitors are expected to venture to the museum this morning.

I wonder, whether Sophia will be one of them.

Socrates, the famed philosopher of classical Hellas was very much on her mind as we broke off our discussion last evening. Little did she know, that I had been witness to his final hour. Socrates, whom the oracle of Delphi had decreed to be the wisest man of his time, had been tried and found guilty of defying the gods and corrupting the youth of Athens. There was joy among his critics, when his verdict was announced, but open anger among his friends and supporters. Rumors began circulating that several of his pupils were arranging for him to flee the city.

Personally, I could not believe how a keen and perceptive man like Socrates would have no faith in the gods. He even doubted the existence of Zeus! The fact that the gods blessed and protected only those who honored them, was common knowledge in Athens. Socrates surely must have known that.

"I made it, Karyatis," Sophia's familiar voice suddenly interrupts my thoughts. "It is bitter cold outside," she adds.

I watch her as she removes several layers of heavy outerwear, and also a matching blue woolen scarf designed to protect her face from the frigid wind.

"You are a brave girl coming in on a day like this."

"It is only a short walk from my studio, and besides, I was anxious to hear more of your story. Your recollections, yesterday, especially your encounters with Goddess Athena left me captivated."

"They were thrilling moments for me, too, Sophia."

"And what do you have for me this morning?"

"I thought I'd start with Socrates' last hour, and also what I recall of the life and times of Plato, his prize pupil."

"Sounds fascinating! I am ready, whenever you are!"

The location of the cell where Socrates was being held was common knowledge in the city. It was hardly surprising then, as news of his scheduled execution reached the *agora* that a large group of men would gather to witness the event. Most were friends and disciples lamenting his pending doom, but present were also several of his critics.

Luck was with me that evening. The city was under the glow of a full moon; my moment to approach and listen.

"He is inside," I heard a man announce sadly, "prepared to die. His impending death does not faze him, he says, for it will bring to light the truth. He is probably drinking the poisonous hemlock at this very moment."

"How very sad," grieved a bystander.

"Does he know that all arrangements have been made? That the guards will look the other way? In a matter of hours he could be a free man on a boat to the island of Crete."

"Yes, but he refuses to leave. He'd rather die than leave Athens, he says. Leaving now would imply guilt. I have always respected the laws of our city, he told his wife Xanthippe, earlier in the evening when she pleaded with him to heed the counsel of his pupils and escape. Should I break them now just because they do not suit me?"

"It's like him," I heard someone observe in a sarcastic, caustic tone. "Always wanting things his way."

"Please, Harilaos. This is hardly the time or place," came back the angry retort from one of Socrates' devoted disciples. "The man is near death and you are humoring him? Have you no fear of the gods?"

"I just don't think that he is someone who deserves to be mourned. This is the man who has denied the existence of the gods, and whose closest associates have included the traitor Alciviades and the tyrant Critias. Need I say more?"

"You have him all wrong, Harilaos. Socrates is a good man, an honest man who spent his entire life exposing ignorance and hypocrisy." The defending voice was that of another pupil. "If he is guilty of anything, it is for his pursuit of truth and justice in all human contacts. This is a remarkable achievement for someone, who never received an education beyond that which we provide to all our boys."

"So many of you are in a hurry to judge him," he continued, "and in the process are ignoring the man's unfailing love for our city, our laws, and institutions. Who cares really who his associates were? Socrates was as true and loyal an Athenian as any of us. I should know, for I fought alongside him in the battles of Potidaea and at Amphipolis. His bravery and endurance on the battlefield will always remain with me."

"He's made too many enemies!" The critical voice again was that of Harilaos. "His persistent questioning of our political institutions, and disdain for our religious beliefs, have left him few friends among the powerful who could now come to his assistance.

"I recall him drilling me once for hours on the subject of bravery. What is bravery, he would ask? Does bravery mean fighting against one who is stronger than you, or does it mean having the courage to back down from such a fight and accept the insults of cowardice that would follow? Does bravery mean turning in your father to the authorities, if he has committed a crime? We all know what bravery is; so did Socrates. Why then, did he feel the need to browbeat me on this subject?"

"He was not browbeating you, Harilaos. Asking questions and seeking answers was his way of searching for the truth. Socrates was always a relentless questioner, but his questions were never shallow or idle. They had a purpose. They aimed to arrive at the truth."

"We all knew of his passion for asking questions." The voice this time was of another critic. "This was not why he was tried. Socrates was charged with insulting the gods, teaching of new gods, and corrupting the youth of Athens. These were grave charges and the jury found him guilty on all counts. I was present at the trial, and I should know."

"So was I, my friend, and I recall that he denied all these charges. As for his sentence, the judges had no desire to condemn him to death; they even asked him what his penalty should be. Everyone had hoped that he would suggest banishment, but he would never agree to leaving his beloved Athens.

"Because of his age he could even have been pardoned for his offenses, if only he would ask for mercy. But he would have none of this. I demand justice, he said, not mercy. Exasperated by his behavior the judges sentenced him to death."

The appearance of a man walking slowly out of the jail entrance and in the direction of the waiting crowd put a quick end to the debate. He could barely contain his grief.

"It is all over," he whispered. "Socrates has taken the poison. He is no more."

"Was he alone?

"Was he alone, when his time came?" asked a disciple, his voice quivering with grief.

"No. Plato was there, and so were several other pupils. Xanthippe had left earlier on order of the guards."

During the years that followed, Sophia, the task of keeping Socrates' theories alive fell upon Plato. The old master had never recorded any of his thoughts, and had it not been for his loyal pupil and disciple Plato, few today would have known of him. His contributions to mankind would have been lost forever.

Plato was a natural for the task. He practiced Socrates' style of investigation, and like his mentor was uncompromising in the pursuit of truth. What is love, he would ask? What is justice? What is truth, while testing his theories and exploring rules of ethical behavior for men to follow. Later in life, Plato established an academy in Athens as a forum for advancing Socrates' ideas among the youth. The academy became the place to be, for any thoughtful young Hellene aspiring to master the finer points of philosophy, science, and political theory.

Plato never entered politics, even though he was expected to do so as the son of an aristocratic Athenian family. A great political theorist himself, he had become disillusioned with the shortcomings of Athenian democracy, and the caliber of some of the persons running the city. He elected instead to become a teacher. Among his illustrious pupils was Aristotle, who later became the celebrated mentor and colleague of the Macedonian prince Alexander. It had been Alexander's father, King Philip, who insisted that Aristotle instruct the young prince from his earliest youth, and expose him to all aspects of science, literature, political theory, and philosophy.

"King Philip, Karyatis, is another of Edward's favorite historical figures. More so than Alexander the Great. Edward must have read every biography and book written on the Macedonian monarch, and has made repeated pilgrimages to his newly discovered tomb in Vergina. He finds the man to be fascinating and in the same class as Bismarck, Garibaldi and other famous nation builders in history."

"Edward and I have similar tastes, Sophia. I too was very fond of Philip, back then.

"Incidentally, I hope to see this friend of yours one of these days. You will bring him around, won't you, when he returns from Washington?"

"Of course, I will. Besides, Edward is a member of the museum's trustees, and as such spends a great deal of time in this building. I'll bring him around during one of his visits here."

From the very start, Sophia, long before the Macedonian king set his sights on Athens, he was the subject of much debate in the city. Sparta, many complained, may have won the war, but it was the wizardry of Philip of Macedonia that was slowly eroding the power and influence of Athens, relegating it to the status of just another city-state.

The man has but one goal would charge Demosthenes, Philip's most passionate critic in Athens, to conquer all of Hellas, and to rule it from his capital city of Pella.

To be sure, there were voices also in Athens that were a lot less critical. The Macedonian king, they argued, is not after territory. His aim is to unite the cities of Hellas and lead them in a Pan-Hellenic campaign against our arch rival Persia. Philip cannot possibly succeed in this grandiose undertaking as long as infighting keeps tearing apart the various city states.

There is nothing, they would argue, in the man's record to raise undue alarm. All of Philip's accomplishments, his military strength and political cohesion of his kingdom, have been the result of hard work and zeal. The Macedonian king has overcome internal enemies and pretenders to his throne, and has secured his borders with Epiros and Thrace. And in a totally unexpected move, he succeeded in having Thessaly, the most prosperous region in central Hellas, elect him as its commander.

We are next, bemoaned many others. With the combined

forces of Macedonia and Thessaly assembled just beyond our neighboring city of Thebes, how long before we too will get a taste of Philip's machinations?

Needless to say, Sophia, all this talk about Philip and of his plans for a campaign against Persia made me extremely nervous. Was Athens becoming embroiled again in a dangerous far-off campaign, I wondered? Had the blunder of the Sicilian campaign already been forgotten? What is it about this city that makes it seek out foreign adventures? From that day forward, I kept my eyes and ears open for any talk that concerned the Macedonian king.

"It is Demosthenes, it's Demosthenes," I heard a young man shout to his friends one afternoon, as they lingered aimlessly in the vicinity of the Propylaea. "He is heading to the Pnyx to address the assembly. Hurry! We don't want to miss him."

Everyone quickly followed his lead, but one.

"You're not coming?" inquired Hippias of his friend Aristovoulos.

"No, I don't really care to," he answered curtly. "I am not all that anxious to hear Demosthenes again."

"You are not?"

"I am aware that he is a great orator, and I admire his technique for delivering a speech. I don't share his views, however. The man is so possessed with hatred for King Philip, he totally ignores the fundamental interests of our city and those of all of Hellas for that matter."

"I am not sure I follow you, Aristovoulos."

"I mean, the hopeless disarray of the city-states of Hellas, and their tendency of constantly warring against each other. All that Philip is trying to do is bring everyone together; unite us all against Persia, our common enemy."

"I can't believe that you are saying this, my friend. Philip is a megalomaniac, blinded by ambition. His so-called dream of a Pan-Hellenic crusade against Persia, is nothing more than a ploy to acquire more territory and increase Macedonia's military might."

"Still, many city-states have accepted his hegemony on their own, Hippias. They were not bribed or coerced into doing so. They have welcomed Philip as their ally and protector, against our more powerful neighbor the Persians."

"I am afraid, Aristovoulos, you are wrong again. Philip's incursions into central Hellas have been littered with dead Hellenes, destroyed cities, and women and children taken into exile. Nothing "unifying" about that!

"Then, too, we are a democracy, remember? Why should we collaborate with a tyrant?"

Listening to the two young men argue, it soon became clear to me that neither was prepared to give ground.

"I agree. Philip is a monarch and, as such, alien to our democratic traditions," continued Aristovoulos. "But he has given no evidence of planning to change our form of government, or to humble our city in any way. Why listen to Demosthenes and allow ourselves to become embroiled in yet another war? At most, Philip wants Athens to become a dependable ally, so that he may turn his attention eastward. That's not so bad, is it?"

As the group of young men began mingling with the throng of fellow Athenians heading toward the Pnyx, the melodious voice from the podium was unmistakable. Demosthenes, the city's preeminent orator, and most outspoken critic of King Philip was addressing the anxious crowd. He did not temper his words.

"Citizens of Athens," he continued in a ringing voice. "Our city is in mortal danger. One after another our allies have fallen to the Macedonian tyrant, and are now being victimized by him; Methone, Pherae, Pegasae, to mention a few, are now his to exploit. Does anyone possibly believe, that this master of intrigue and bribery is about to end his conquests any day soon? Of course not. Let me assure you, Philip of Macedonia will continue on his path of aggression as long as our policy toward him is one of apathy.

"Yes, my fellow Athenians, I said apathy to his devious and insidious ways.

"Some among you have suggested, that we should reach an accommodation with him.

"An accommodation with Philip? Even the thought is preposterous. We are a democracy with freedoms guaranteed to all our citizens. How could we possibly collaborate with one whose power is rooted in greed and violence? Tyrants, like Philip, are enemies of freedom and opponents of law. Peoples' lives must be based on truth and justice, and this applies to everyone, including our Macedonian brothers. They will tire before long, of the misery and hardship of constant warfare to which their ruthless leader has exposed them."

Demosthenes' message was sweeping through the crowd like a gust of raw wind. His melodious voice, accompanied by rousing gestures, was magnifying the effect of his eloquent words. As a young man he had practiced this technique to strengthen his oratorical powers, often by shouting against the surf, and orating by placing pebbles in his mouth to overcome a speech impediment.

"It is time my fellow citizens," he concluded, "time to defend Athens; time to defend Hellas. We must prepare for war against Philip. He is an irreconcilable enemy. Even if the entire world submits to his slavery, we alone must stand tall and fight him."

"Did Demosthenes carry the day, Karyatis?" interrupted Sophia.

"He sure did. He convinced his fellow citizens to join Thebes in an alliance against Philip. What happened next, however, will really surprise you."

All of a sudden, men in uniforms unlike those worn by Athenian warriors, and speaking a dialect quite different from the polished language spoken in Athens, began appearing on the Acropolis. They were of course Macedonian soldiers.

But surprisingly, Philip's soldiers did not behave at all like occupiers, even though they had every right to do so, having just trounced the Athenians and their allies from Thebes at the battle of Cheronaea. On their visits to the Acropolis, they were in total awe at what they saw, and I could tell from their many favorable comments that they had never before seen such beautiful art or temples.

The people of Athens had mixed feelings about the Macedonians. On one hand, they looked down on them as being culturally inferior, on the other, they admired their discipline and brilliance of their military leaders. They were aware, of course, that the Macedonians as direct descendants of Achilles and of the demigod Hercules were fellow Hellenes, no different than say Corinthians or Naxians. But it was their young Prince Alexander whom they found most puzzling. He had beaten them decisively at Cheronaea, had in effect put an end to the Athenian empire, yet he treated their city with such chivalry and generosity as to be totally mystifying.

I saw a clear demonstration of this one afternoon, Sophia, when a young Athenian just back from the battle of Cheronaea met a friend not far from where I was standing. Their discussion centered on none other than Alexander. I'll try to retell the story, as best as I can recall it.

"We are safe! Athens is safe," exclaimed the young man jubilantly, as he gazed at the tranquil city below. Leaning against a nearby rock, with his brown *himation* soiled with blood and his right arm supported by a makeshift sling, he gave every indication of being a *hoplite* just back from the front.

"Timotheos," he remarked, turning in the direction of the young man standing next to him. "Do you realize how very fortunate we are? We provoked Alexander as much as anyone. At Cheronaea he totally devastated our forces, yet he has allowed our city to remain intact. Not one building will be razed or otherwise be demolished".

"Yes, Ephorus, Athena's divine power has spared our city one more time."

"But, poor Thebes! It is paying dearly for opposing the Macedonian king. Its leaders have been summarily executed and their property confiscated. Captives are being sold into slavery and Theban war dead (contrary to Hellenic customs and traditions) can only be buried on payment of a high fee.

"They should not have listened to Demosthenes," moaned Ephorus. "Thebes and our city, too, could have reached an honorable accommodation with Philip. It would have spared a lot of suffering all around.

"There was no way really that we could have prevailed at Cheronaea. The two armies were about equal in size, but the Macedonians could not be matched in leadership. For years King Philip had been improving his war-fighting capability. While we deliberated on how best to respond to his challenge, he was busily perfecting the readiness of his troops, especially that dread military formation of his, known as the phalanx.

"I'll never forget the moment that I first came face to face with it. It was awesome! Those enormously long pikes staring at us, and with the entire Macedonian formation moving as a single man! Our short weapons were absolutely no match.

"For a while, we tried to confront the unusual formation by modifying our tactics. But then, out of nowhere, the Macedonian cavalry appeared on the battlefield, with Alexander astride his horse Bucephalus. A total rout of our troops followed, with Demosthenes himself being among the first to flee. As for this arm wound of mine, it was caused by an aide to the Macedonian prince, who stabbed me when I tried foolishly to resist his onslaught."

"Praise the gods, Ephorus, for sparing your life. At the *agora* last evening, there was talk of about 1,000 or so of our *hoplites* having lost their lives during the battle. Another 2,000 were taken prisoners by the Macedonians."

"It could have been a lot worse."

"Still, it is amazing my friend, how kind and generous Alexander has turned out to be toward our city. In exchange for our pledge to join the League of Corinth, which will be the alliance of the city-states in the war against Persia, he has promised not to defile our city. We can remain free and independent of Macedonian rule. He has even allowed us to retain political control over the islands of Lemnos, Imbros, and Samos."

"I hear, that even Demosthenes agrees that Alexander's terms are extremely generous," remarked Ephorus.

"Yes. What has touched everyone in the city is the young prince's decision to free all Athenian prisoners taken at Cheronaea, and to return the bodies of the men who fell in the battle. Alexander himself will lead the honor guard for the dead, along with Antipatros, his father's most trusted general. And would you believe it? He has given Demosthenes permission to deliver the oration for the dead at the funeral."

"Our city fathers are doing well, Timotheos, responding to Alexander's leniency by making him an honorable citizen of Athens. I hear that plans are also under way to erect a statue of his father, King Philip, in the *agora.*"

"Personally, I see no reason why we shouldn't. He is after all the undisputed master of Hellas. And you know what? I don't mind it a bit!"

"Neither do I," added Ephorus.

The euphoria did not last, Sophia. "He's dead! He's dead! Philip has been murdered," I heard a Macedonian warrior shout one morning, as he approached a group of his countrymen lingering nearby. I strained to hear the astonishing news.

Apparently, King Philip had been assassinated by one of his bodyguards during festivities on the occasion of the wedding of one of his daughters. His body was cremated in Aegae and a majestic tomb was being prepared in Vergina in his honor.

"Who would want to do such a horrible thing?" I heard someone ask.

"There are suspicions," answered another, "that Queen Olympias, the mother of Alexander, might be involved. She's been jealous of the king taking on a seventh wife recently, a Macedonian maiden named Cleopatra. Olympias was fearful that Cleopatra would provide Philip with a male heir to replace Alexander. We'll never know the truth, though. The assassin himself was killed by some of the king's other bodyguards."

The sudden news left me distraught and deep in thought. Will Alexander assume the throne now? In the past, he had been kind to Athens out of respect for the city's status as the leading center of learning in all of Hellas. Will he continue feeling this way in the future? And what about King Philip's planned campaign against Persia? Will it go on as scheduled?

"You worried too much, Karyatis," remarked Sophia, part jesting, part serious. "One can never be sure of the future!"

"I recognize that, but what would you have done in my position? Here I was, unlike all other statues, able to understand what was happening around me, but unable to control my fate the way that you humans can."

"As a statue you were pretty safe. No one would have hurt you."

"I am not so sure of that, Sophia. Alexander was known for being bad-tempered, more times than one. Do you recall the punishment that he exacted on poor Thebes when it revolted against him the second time?"

"No, I don't recall the incident."

"I'll let Efterpe tell it in her own words. She was one of the fortunate few who was able to escape Thebes and the wrath of Alexander."

"We should never have listened to Demosthenes," the young woman moaned repeatedly, as she began seeking shelter for herself and her four young wards, amidst several large slabs of marble behind the temple of Athena Nike.

"Beautiful Thebes is no more, all because of him."

She paused briefly in front of a small tool shed filled with hammers, chisels, and other construction implements left behind by a crew. "We should be safe here," she remarked.

They made a dismal sight: five truly impoverished children, in their bare feet, completely dispirited by lack of food and water.

She reached into the stained sack hanging loosely from her shoulder and removed a large brown bedspread. "Lydia," she instructed the oldest child, "here, try to keep them warm while I go out in search of food".

Later, as they all drew close together over a humble meal of goat meat and grapes, left over from the evening sacrifices, I heard Lydia ask:

"Efterpe, who is Demosthenes and why should not have listened to him?"

"He is an Athenian, Lydia, known for his opposition to

King Philip. He is the one who convinced our leaders to form a rebellion against Alexander and attack the Macedonian garrison in our city.

"Demosthenes had spread rumors that Alexander had died, and like fools we believed him. How were we to know that the Macedonian King was well and healthy? That he was in his capital city, planning the campaign against Persia?

"When Alexander appeared like lightning in front of our city walls and demanded our surrender, our leaders turned to our friends for help. But Athens and Sparta, who had secretly conspired with us against the Macedonian king hesitated. So did our other neighbors. We were forced to confront him alone.

"After he had stormed and taken our city, Alexander asked our neighbors the Boeotians what our fate should be. Raze the city, they urged him. Get rid of Thebes once and forever, and sell all remaining Thebans into slavery!

"So much for our good neighbors!

"As you noticed I am sure, while we were leaving Thebes, Alexander carried out the sentence in full, leveling our entire city and sparing from destruction only the sanctuaries to the gods, and the house of his friend the poet Pindar. He is probably selling the surviving population into slavery at this very moment."

"What is to become of us now, Efterpe," wondered the young maiden.

"We are safe here, Lydia. Do not worry. By the grace of the gods we made it into Athens, a city known for its warm welcome and hospitality toward those in need. Have no fear, we will be taken care of here."

"Karyatis? I am truly becoming disenchanted with all these horrid stories of wars, misery, and massacres. Did not Athens, didn't you ever enjoy a period of extended peace, when there were no invading armies, insurrections, or conflict?"

"We did. Alexander's brutal punishment of Thebes had a sobering effect on everyone. Soon, all active resistance to the Macedonian rule ceased, and the young king was recognized as the supreme leader of all of Hellas. Several thousand Athenian men in fact, along with warriors from many other city states, joined his army. Peace finally had arrived."

Athens fared well, Sophia, during the years of Alexander's rule. On his orders, the city was freed of all forms of Macedonian control, thus allowing it to establish once again a democratic form of government. With the return of peace, the Athenian navy began reasserting its leading trading role in the Adriatic Sea, economic prosperity returned to much of Attica, and construction of new buildings blossomed in the *agora.* The academies established by Aristotle and Plato continued to gain in fame and prominence, during the entire period, and scores of youth from all over Hellas traveled to Athens to take advantage of the unique opportunity presented by them for the study of philosophy and political theory.

As for the Macedonian king, stories began circulating that he had launched his campaign against Persia, and that after crossing Asia Minor, Syria, and a large desert, he had reached a land known as Egypt where he was received with great acclaim. Near the delta of the Nile River, he had established a new city named after himself. Alexandria, the new city, some said would eventually rival Memphis and Athens as a center of philosophy, literature, and the sciences.

Barely old enough when he assumed the throne, Alexander led a formidable army in a crusade to avenge the invasion of Hellas by Persian forces, during the reigns of Kings Darius and Xerxes, and as events later proved, to advance Hellenic culture and civilization deep into Asia.

In battle, on his great charger Bucephalus, and protected by a sacred shield from the Trojan War, Alexander was fearless.

You look surprised, Sophia. Yes, Alexander was able to acquire this shield when he paused in Troy to pray to the gods at the start of his Asian campaign. The shield remained with him to the very end.

Success crowned his every military encounter, and through it all, he kept faith never forgetting his affection for Athens. After the battle of the Granicus river, for instance, he stripped three hundred enemy dead of their armor, and had it dispatched to our city as an offering to goddess Athena. It was kept on display by the statue of Athena Promachos, on the Acropolis, for a very long time.

Alexander's humanity toward Athens notwithstanding, a great many Athenians became disillusioned as news began to reach the city of the cruelty displayed by his men toward some of his enemies.

When the port of Tyre, for instance, challenged the young king and lost, most members of its garrison were slaughtered, and the city itself was razed, despite Alexander's earlier promise of amnesty.

News, years later, of the sudden death of Alexander in far-off Babylon left Athenians and all of Hellas stunned. According to reports by soldiers who had served under his command and made it safely back, Alexander had just returned from a campaign deep into Asia, when he suddenly was taken ill. His body was transferred to Egypt by one of his generals. A grandiose building was erected in Alexandria, the city that he had founded, and his body was displayed there for all to see.

"Next time you are with Edward, Sophia, you may want to ask him, whether Alexander's body can still be viewed in Alexandria?"

"I doubt it very much, Karyatis. Not after all those years."

"What could have happened to it?"

"Frankly, I don't know."

"Alexander left no heir. At his deathbed his generals begged him to designate a successor. "To whom do you bequeath what you have acquired", they asked him. "To the strongest", he replied in his last breath. When his military commanders were unable to agree on any one successor, they decided to carve up the empire amongst them. General Antipatros became in the process the ruler of most of Hellas, including the city of Athens."

Before long, Sophia, many of the Athenian *hoplites* that had joined Alexander in his campaign into Asia began returning home.

"I joined Alexander's army in Memphis," I heard the old *hoplite* announce, to the large crowd of anxious men and women in the *agora* one evening. Draped in his military cloak, sword and shield still on hand, he was among a small group of Athenian warriors on the latest *trireme* from Tyre. He was along in years and weary, but his walk was proud and he had the demeanor of a conquering hero returning home.

"Please brothers and sisters," he pleaded above the clamor of the questions being shouted at him. "I will try to answer as many of your questions, as I can. I know how anxious you are for news on your loved ones serving in Asia."

"Did you ever happen to come across one by the name of Democides, from Chalkis, the son of Neotarcus?" inquired a clearly despondent woman. "What about Stasikrates ... Stasikrates, the son of Melanthios from Lavrion? We have not had any news from him since he left."

"Do you recall ever meeting Neotarcus, the son of Androtion from Aegina?"

"No, I am sorry," replied the old warrior in a melancholy, compassionate voice. "I am not familiar with any of these men. Perhaps, others on board our ship can provide you with some details about them. I have had very limited contact with Athenians serving under Alexander, being assigned duty at his palace in Babylon, while most Athenians served on the front."

"Were you with Alexander when he invaded India," asked a bystander. "What in the name of Zeus did he want way out there? In India, of all places?"

The old warrior smiled. "Perhaps, if you give me a chance to explain.

"I had barely arrived in Memphis," he continued, "when the king ordered the army to leave Egypt, and to march on toward the Persian capital. We met no opposition at first, crossing the Euphrates and Tigris rivers without difficulty, but suddenly Darius decided to challenge us. It was there that we first encountered elephants on the field of battle, fighting alongside the Persian cavalry. None of us had ever seen such massive animals before. They were almost impossible to take down!

"Though Darius' forces were far more numerous than ours, Alexander's military genius again prevailed. Through a series of skillful maneuvers, he succeeded in opening a major gap in the Persian lines and in neutralizing the Persian cavalry, including Darius' prize elephants. A complete rout followed, with the Persians fleeing for life and our warriors pursuing and attacking them relentlessly.

"It was not long afterwards that we marched into Babylon, which as many of you know is the largest city of Asia, and also one of Persia's four capitals , along with Persepolis, Susa, and Echatana. Nearly all Persian treasures of gold and silver were kept in Babylon."

"Unbelievable," someone whispered. "Destroying the mighty Persian empire, and getting hold of its treasures! It is all beyond belief."

"These were all brave acts, my friend," I heard a bystander remark. "Is there truth, however, to the reports that Alexander before his death had claimed for himself the title of the Great King of Persia, and that he had married a Persian princess? Also, that his troops after his foray into India had refused to go any further?"

"Yes, much of what you heard is true. But please keep in mind, that Alexander who sat on the throne of Persia was a different person than the youth who had departed Hellas. The deeper into Asia that Alexander pushed, the more his earlier designs of taking revenge on Persia changed. By the time he had reached Babylon, his goal had become one of bringing about a reconciliation between east and west. Toward this end he even took Darius' daughter Barsine as his bride, appointed Persians to key administrative posts in the empire, and even allowed thousands of young Persians to join his army."

"Did he also give the wife of Darius a lavish funeral when she died, and arranged for the education of her son Ochus?"

"He did."

"You mean he became a Persian in all but name?"

"This is a contemptuous comment, and one that I refuse to honor with an answer," snapped back the old man angrily.

"Listen well, my friend," he continued after a brief pause. "Alexander cannot be compared with any other person in history. Since that day in Phrygia, when he drew his sword and sliced the Gordian knot in half, there's been little doubt that the young king was destined to rule the East. It should hardly have come as a surprise. The gods had decreed, that the riches of Asia would lay open to the person able to release the Gordian knot.

"Single-handedly, he created the largest empire the world has ever seen. He conquered Egypt, Persia, and parts of India. He founded numerous new cities. He spread Hellenic civilization deep into Asia. These accomplishments did not happen by chance. Alexander was fully aware of the significance of his mission, and arranged for geographers, historians, map makers, and scientists to accompany his troops and record his every achievement.

"As for him becoming a Persian, nothing could be further from the truth. To the very end, Alexander remained a true Hellene motivated by the single desire to promote Hellenic culture and civilization to parts of the world that until then had not been exposed to. His untimely death has deprived Hellas of its greatest son."

He clearly wanted to say no more.

"On to Megara," he whispered, "to find what's left of my family."

He picked up his pouch of personal belongings, which lay in front of him, and resumed slowly his trek through the *agora* in the direction of the neighboring city, and his home.

"Kind of sad, Karyatis. Alexander's untimely death at the age of thirty-three, robbed Hellas of one of its most visionary leaders."

"It was an amazing achievement Sophia -- spreading Hellenic culture and civilization throughout the ancient world, and making the language spoken in Attica the universal language of the times, all within the span of a few years. And, as the warrior from Megara so vividly confirmed, Alexander's goal in Asia had not been territorial conquest, but the reconciliation of all peoples living in the area."

"Truly noble, Karyatis, and well ahead of his times!"

"Yes."

"How did Hellas react to the news of Alexander's death? Did the peace, which had been imposed after the pillage of Thebes continue?"

"Not for long. An extended period of unrest followed, as Alexander's generals and their successors competed for territory and influence within the empire. For most of the time, Athens stayed clear of all such infighting, succeeding in the process to preserve its independence and democratic form of government. But, on occasion, it could not resist the temptation of rising against its Macedonian rulers."

The first such revolt occurred when news of the death of Alexander reached the city. At the forefront of the anti-Macedonian movement stood Demosthenes again, urging his fellow Athenians to take up arms before a new ruler could consolidate power in the empire. The attempt failed miserably, when Antipatros, who had already assumed command of all of Hellas on the death of Alexander, confronted the rebellious Athenian army in the plains of Attica and defeated it decisively.

Athens paid dearly for its defiance. Demosthenes was banished from the city forever (he subsequently committed suicide), his followers were deprived of their civil rights, and a Macedonian military force was billeted permanently in the city.

Hurt and humiliated by Antipatros, Athens became in the years that followed a pawn in the wars among Alexander's successors. Wisely, it decided to take it all in stride, refusing to take sides but honoring the winners of particular conflicts by erecting statues or establishing altars in their honor.

Many material benefits accrued to Athens from its new posture. Without military commitments or engagements to drain its treasury, prosperity returned. But sadly, the city began also to lose its purity, with the once pious Athenians openly expressing skepticism about the existence of their gods. What offended me particularly, Sophia, was allowing Dimitrios Polyorkitis (he was the son of Antigonos, the ruler of Asia) to use the temple of Athena as his official residence.

Dimitrios spent an entire winter living in the Parthenon, if you can believe that, while Athena's priests and priestesses performed their sacred rites nearby. It was such an atrocious and sacrilegious act; unquestionably my worse memory of the period. The only excuse of the city officials for this desecration was that they were grateful to Dimitrios Polyorkitis for having removed from power the city's earlier tyrannical ruler.

The post-Alexander years were otherwise quite good for Athens. The arts and sciences blossomed and so did Hellenic language and culture. In a strange oddity of history, the less political power and influence Athens possessed, the more important it became as a center of culture and civilization.

But before long, Athens again rose against the Macedonians, and again their rebellion ended in defeat. Their target this time was King Philip the Fifth. Unsure of their ability to overcome his military power, the Athenians committed a strategic error: they asked Rome for help, which of course it readily agreed to offer. Eventually, the Athenians were able to defeat Philip's army, but the Romans who had been instrumental in the victory, had plans of their own. General Flamininus, the leader of the Roman forces, thereupon declared on behalf of Rome that all of Hellas was now free from Macedonia. The declaration, needless to say, gave Rome the excuse to begin interfering in the affairs of Hellas.

Not long afterwards, when the son of Philip the Fifth failed to reassert Macedonian control over the lost territories, Hellas in effect became a province of Rome. The Roman Senate sealed the new order by appointing Salpikion Gallos, as the first Roman ruler of Athens.

"This in effect was the end of Hellas?" pondered Sophia.

"Yes, of the Hellas I knew during the classical times. I hear that there is a new Hellas now, far from here, where my sisters are."

"Yes Karyatis. And I have not forgotten that you wish to join them some day."

"Not just some day, Sophia, but some day soon! Do you hear me? Soon!"

"Yes, Karyatis. But this is not the time or place for this subject. It is too complex for us to take up now. I promise, though, in due time we will discuss it".

"Must you leave now?"

"Yes. Edward will be calling soon, and with the time differential between Washington and London, I don't want to miss his call. I am also meeting later some friends for dinner to plan a surprise 40th birthday celebration for my former university roommate, Elizabeth. We are thinking of starting our evening with dinner in an 'in' restaurant and then see a show. These days, women go out a lot without men. Quite different from the early days that you remember in Athens."

V

A PROVINCE OF ROME

I wonder where Sophia is this morning. It is almost noontime, and still no sign of her. As she was leaving last evening rushing home to receive a phone call from Edward, she gave no indication of being late today, or not coming in at all. Could something be wrong?

Here I go worrying again.

All my life it seems, I have been a worrier. How could I not be, facing the kind of uncertainties that I did? Such as when the Hellas that I knew and loved ceased to exist? Rome, everyone said, would be in charge from now on. A Roman official had been appointed to rule Athens.

This is the same Rome, that had declared earlier that henceforth all of Hellas would be free of Macedonian rule. But general Flamininus, who had made the pledge on behalf of Rome, had spoken only half the truth. As it turned, out Roman rule soon replaced that of Macedonia.

But the Macedonians despite their awkward ways were at least fellow Hellenes, while the Romans were not. Why should Roman rule be preferable to that of Macedonia?

And how could I, a simple statue, not worry in the face of what the Romans had done not long ago to Corinth? Beautiful Corinth, with dozens of exquisite temples and public buildings, and for a long time one of the largest cities of Hellas, had resisted Rome's demands that it dissolve the Achaian League of which it had been the leader. In response, the Roman consul Lucius Mummius leveled the city, killing its men, and selling its women and children into slavery. Innumerable statues from the city's sanctuaries were plundered; some even found their way to Rome. The devastation of the once glorious city was so complete, only squatters occupied the site when Julius Caesar decided to reestablish it many years later.

The sacking of Corinth had the desired effect for Rome, however. No one questioned any longer who the new masters of Hellas were.

At the new Corinth, a man called Paul, a Hellenized Jew who hailed from the city of Tarsus, arrived many years later to preach the gospel of a new God. He had selected Corinth for his message, he said, because the city under Roman rule had become especially licentious, with thousands of prostitutes roaming the streets and even residing in the temples of the gods.

I had heard Paul speak a few years earlier, when accompanied by two disciples he addressed a crowd in the *agora* with the same message. His God, he said, had come down from heaven to save mankind, was later crucified and in three days rose from death.

Paul's words bewildered me. I remember thinking: the nerve of the man, preaching such contemptuous lies! Isn't he afraid of the wrath of Zeus?

He had started his mission in Asia Minor, preaching his gospel in Troy, on the very spot that Achilles and Alexander the Great had earlier sacrificed to the gods. Next, he headed to Philippi, Thessaloniki, Amphipolis, and to Verea. His fellow Jews generally ignored him. but in an act that must have infuriated the gods many Hellenes flocked to him. Included was a prominent Athenian justice of the Arios Pagos, by the name of Dionysos, who later became a high official of the new religion.

In his first address in Athens, Paul accused the city of being given to idolatry. Why do you maintain all these monuments, he asked. There is but one God of whom I speak, the One who rules in heaven, not all these gods whom you worship.

This kind of talk did not go over well with the leaders of the city, and soon Paul was summoned to appear before the Arios Pagos. He was charged with promoting a new and outlandish deity.

Little did I know then, that what Paul was preaching would eventually take hold and become the basis of a new religion, one which ultimately would replace the time honored faith to the Olympian gods, that had been venerated by Hellenes through the ages.

"Athenians," I recall him address the assembled crowd on the Arios Pagos. "I perceive that in all things you are a very religious people. As I was passing through your city, I even found an altar with the inscription "To the Unknown God".

"I came to proclaim to you this one God, whom you worship without knowing who He is. He is a God of love and mercy, who sent His only begotten Son to earth to save mankind from sin."

Loud laughter repeatedly interrupted Paul's speech. The ridicule and sneering became even more pronounced, when he announced that the Son of God had risen from the dead and would return one day to judge the living and the dead, and that his Kingdom would have no end.

How could anyone believe such absurdity, I wondered? The people of Athens certainly would not. They burned their dead, and as everyone knew a human body that had been destroyed by fire could not be made to live again.

Disillusioned, and with only a few adherents to show for his efforts, Paul departed Athens a few days later. But his message did not depart with him. Gradually, it provided the bedrock on which the new religion flourished.

The giggling, chuckling sounds of several young girls, dressed in attractive brown uniforms of a private London school, suddenly interrupt my thoughts. A museum official, who is escorting them through my gallery, is attempting to make them focus on the business at hand.

"The statue in front of us,"... he begins.

Same distortions as before: "...The Caryatid was brought here from the Acropolis, in Athens, etc, etc, etc...through the years it has been carefully preserved by the British Museum, etc, etc,... had it not been brought here, it could have suffered from lack of care in Athens... etc, etc."

Walking behind the guide, close enough to be able to listen

to his narration is the familiar silhouette of Sophia. I can tell by her facial expression that she is troubled by what she is hearing.

She looks up at me, as the group of the young girls moves on.

"Don't mind him," she whispers. "He's is just mouthing the official line of the museum."

Her comment pleases me, but also leaves me a bit bewildered. Has Sophia, hopefully, come around to my point of view?

"I know," I answer meekly. "I try not to listen to him whenever he speaks."

I watch as she removes her wet leather coat, uncovers her canvas, and prepares in her own orderly manner to resume work. A package of sorts is resting on the stool beside her.

"You were late this morning!"

"I know. I had several errands to run, and also made brief stops on the way in at the Museum's bookstore and at the Department of Greek and Roman Antiquities," she volunteers.

"Greek and Roman Antiquities? What for?"

"My friend Martha works there. I wanted to check out with her a rumor that has been circulating among art circles. A small section of ancient relief has reportedly been stolen, over the weekend, from the grounds of the museum."

"Stolen from this very building? I can't believe it! It wasn't part of the Parthenon collection, was it?

"No, no, it was not. It was from a panel of the Temple of Apollo in Bassae. According to Martha, the museum officials are not sure as yet, whether they are dealing with a case of theft, an act of vandalism, or just a prank by a mischievous kid."

"What difference does it make, Sophia?" I sense anger building inside me. "The museum allowed a stranger to walk out with a piece of the world's most valued art. It is inexcusable."

"I agree, Karyatis."

"The theft, if this is what it was, demolishes of course the argument that Hellenic art is safer in the British Museum, than it would be at a museum back in Athens."

"It does."

"Thank you for agreeing with me. If you get any later news, will you please let me know? I'd love to hear how the museum will react to the event."

"Of course.

"Closer to home, Karyatis, what have you been up to this morning?

"Been busy organizing my thoughts on the Roman period in Hellas."

"The Roman rule, oh yes -- our lesson plan for today."

"There is a lot to tell on this subject. Rome ruled Hellas for a very long time. There is the story of the rise of Christianity, and how it eventually edged out the time-honored faith to the Olympian gods, the wholesale theft of Hellenic art by Roman emperors and other imperial functionaries, and invasions by barbarians, and much more.

"Where would you like me to begin?"

"This being Sunday, Karyatis, why don't we start with the story of Christianity."

"Forgive me for asking, Sophia. Are you a Christian?"

"Yes."

"Such an admission would have made me quite angry

years ago."

"I understand. But, times have changed. Why don't you go on with your story."

"All right."

Christianity, Sophia, did not take hold overnight in Roman Hellas. In fact, belief in the one God about whom Paul from Tarsus had spoken earlier spread very slowly. Persecution by the authorities had kept down the number of Christians for a while, necessitating the few believers to practice their faith in private homes and catacombs. But, as new converts joined their ranks and Christianity was given official status within the empire, Christians became increasingly bolder. New type structures known as *ecclesies* (churches) made their appearance, and local artists adorned them with representations of the life of Christ, his Crucifixion, and Resurrection. Athenians who believed in the one God began identifying themselves as Christians, and worshipped in *ecclesies* amid much chanting and incense burning.

As the new religion grew in strength, Athenians began to pay less and less homage to the Olympian gods. They defiled their statues and temples, often taking them down for use as construction materials for bridges, roads, and waterworks. The destruction carried out by Christians, on the temples and sanctuaries honoring the Olympian gods, was enormous. It probably outdid that of the Persians and Romans during their original conquests of Hellas. When the old temples were not destroyed outright, they were converted into *ecclesies*. Christians loved to worship in large *ecclesies*. The greater their belief in their God, the larger and more elaborate their *ecclesies*.

Much of the credit for the success of Christianity rests with the Roman authorities. Christianity was barely known when Emperor Constantine decreed that it could be practiced freely, even though he himself did not join the new faith until his deathbed. As an aside, Sophia, I did see Emperor Constantine when he visited the Acropolis with his entourage, soon after he had been proclaimed Augustus and assumed his throne. The accompanying imperial pomp and regalia notwithstanding, he gave me the impression of a very modest, unassuming person. An elderly lady that was in his retinue, I discovered later, was his mother Eleni, whom Christians have elevated to sainthood. The emperor paused in front of me and my sisters for several minutes, and continued to examine us carefully while a local functionary recited for him the history of the various temples on the Acropolis. My opinion of Constantine, however, changed in a flash, when I learned that he too, like many other Roman emperors before him, had ordered several works of art to be removed from the Acropolis and shipped to the Imperial capital of Constantinople.

Constantine's edict ended the persecution of the Christians in the empire, but sadly gave rise to the oppression of those who still honored the Olympian gods. Later edicts, especially by Emperor Theodosios, forbade the worshipping of the old gods and ordered that their sanctuaries be closed. Animal sacrifices were outlawed by punishment of death, and all art in their honor was ordered destroyed. Even the Olympic games, a time-honored tradition in Hellas, were declared pagan celebrations and ordered terminated. Christian bishops were especially fanatical in their pursuit of nonbelievers, accusing them of worshipping pagan gods and conducting sacrifices in secret, even in instances when the slaughter of animals was merely part of a family feast. Rural areas suffered especially, with monks and other Christian clergy harassing non-Christians, destroying their temples and confiscating their lands.

The prosecution of nonbelievers ultimately brought the desired effect. Belief in the Olympian gods waned throughout Hellas, and Christianity blossomed. Nothing symbolized this more than the conversion to a Christian church of the holy temple of the Parthenon. Overnight, the house of Athena Parthenos on the Acropolis became the Church of Panaghia Athiniotissa. The name Panaghia, Sophia, refers to the Virgin Mary, who gave birth to Christ.

"Yes, I know. I am a Christian, remember?"

Several changes were made in the interior of the new church, including the building of an apse at the east end to accommodate the Christian altar. The statue of Athena which had already been stolen by infidels -- I'll have to tell you more about this later -- was replaced by a large icon of the Virgin Mary. Before long, the church was designated as the Cathedral of Athens, and a marble throne removed from the Theater of Dionysos was positioned in the center of the temple for use by the local bishop.

"Did you actually witness the removal of the statue of Athena Parthenos from the temple? To this day archaeologists and historians are unsure who might have been responsible for its theft. There are various theories. One of them holds that it was moved to Constantinople to decorate Constantine's Forum, but no definitive proof has ever been found on that."

"It was stolen, all right. I saw it happening, Sophia. Vile

persons, truly despicable, about a dozen of them, invaded the sacred Parthenon one evening and carried off the statue. They took it down under the cover of darkness, wrapped it quickly in a white cloth, and placed it in a wooden canister. They were gone before anyone could react; not that anyone really tried to stop them. For seven centuries, this gigantic statue of Athena in gold and ivory had reigned supreme in the temple's inner sanctum where no mortal was allowed to enter."

"No one tried to stop them?"

"Absolutely no one! The wailing by a few of the priestesses, on duty at the temple, was the only protest that I could hear.

"It was truly a sacrilegious and contemptuous act, Sophia. I thought so when I saw it happening, and I still do so many centuries later."

"The removal of the statue, Karyatis, and the conversion of the Parthenon into a Christian church must have been traumatic experiences for you."

"Of course. they were. Before long even I was becoming resigned to the fact that the old gods were no more."

"Even Athena?"

"Sadly, yes, even Athena."

I saw her for the last time on the morning that the Church of Panaghia Athiniotissa was to be consecrated as the city's Cathedral. For days leading to that event, I watched with obvious curiosity, but also apprehension, as dozens of Christian clergy in long black robes busied themselves preparing the entire area surrounding the Parthenon for something obviously big. Statues of Olympian gods were removed or concealed behind white curtains, Christian icons, crosses and other symbols were brought in, and a wide carpet was laid out at the north entrance. Strange chants could be heard at all hours emanating from inside the temple.

"I cannot stand it any longer in there," whispered suddenly the young woman, sitting on a marble slab not far from where I was standing. She was wearing a white *peplos* over a long frock, typical of the apparel worn then by most Athenian women.

"All these bearded men in their black robes," she continued, "running around the temple crossing themselves, and chanting strange hymns. I just cannot bear it any longer."

Confused by her disguise, and unaware at first that it was indeed Goddess Athena, I listened quietly while she continued her wailing.

"This is what I get after all that I've done for this city? I am being thrown away like an unwanted and dried out plant?"

How was I to know that it was her? Both her earlier appearances before me had been truly pyrotechnic events. Not this time however; there were no flashes of blinding light, or mighty winds to announce her arrival. In fact, her overall bearing was so lifeless, it took a lot of speaking on her part for me to become convinced that this indeed had been the goddess.

"How dare they evict me from my own home, Karyatis? Evict me, the daughter of Zeus, the one that He gave birth to without the help of a woman? Mount Olympus shook violently, and the gods watched in utter astonishment on the day of my birth, when on Zeus' orders and amidst a shower of gold leaves from above I leaped from his head in full armor. "I proclaim you my Goddess of Wisdom," he announced amidst the splendor of the moment, "and as proof of my special affection for you, I am presenting you with this gift. Use it cautiously, use it wisely," he added.

"It was the thunderbolt, Karyatis, the one that you had seen me use so many times afterwards!"

"It frightened me, Athena, whenever you did," I recall telling her. "Not knowing whether your anger was directed at me, or someone else nearby."

"In fact, it had been directed at you quite a few times! Like the day that I saw you in the *agora* listening to that apostate, Paul from Tarsus."

Not wanting to reopen old wounds, I changed the subject. "What will happen to you now," I asked.

"I have no place to go," she whispered. "On the Acropolis, where once I ruled supreme and where no other deity had a say, I am being treated now like a pariah. In Megara, Phokis, Corinth, Tegea, and Argos, too, where not long ago I was worshipped as protector and defender of the people, my name now is all but forgotten. They have found a new goddess now, in Panaghia Athiniotissa.

"They no longer need me. What an ungrateful people!" I heard her sighing, as she began the slow descent from the Acropolis. "My unfailing love for them, my devotion, my fervor for everything Athenian, are forgotten...."

"That was it? Did you ever see her again?"

"Never."

"She deserved a lot better, Karyatis. I am appalled at the way the people of Athens discarded her," I hear Sophia declare, her usually serene disposition abruptly being overtaken by rising anger.

I pause momentarily. "Is there a problem, Sophia?" I ask. "Suddenly, you seem upset and distracted. Would you prefer that I stop?"

"No. No. I'll be O.K. Please, Karyatis, continue. For a brief moment I had a strange sensation. I felt a rush of strange images... the Parthenon barren without her... wailing priestesses nearby...and me, curiously close to it all. It was quite a bizarre experience....

"I am O.K. now," Sophia repeats. "Please go on with your story. What was life like under Rome?"

"In Athens or in the rest of Hellas?"

"You mean there was a difference?"

"Yes, there was".

The Roman occupation, Sophia, marked Hellas' final decline. Ravaged by near continuous wars among the various city-states, between city-states and Macedonia, Rome and Macedonia, and invasions by barbarians from the north, Hellas finally fell exhausted, bereft of any political or economic power. Her population declined, the countryside was emptied, and its economy shattered. Surprisingly, however, conditions in Athens were much better.

I think I'll let Andronikos, a famed historian and political theorist of that period tell the story. A native of Athens, Andronikos was an acknowledged friend of Rome, who used his academy in a suburb of the city to work for the improvement of relations between Rome and Hellas. His fellow Athenians, uncertain of his views, generally kept him at a distance -- but not the Romans. They loved his savvy and political knowhow and flocked to his classes in very large numbers.

It was during one of my nocturnal excursions into the city, Sophia, when I happened to come across a large gathering of young men. My curiosity got the better of me, so I decided to join the waiting crowd. I am glad that I did. It was my first encounter with Andronikos. From the very outset he mesmerized me, not only by his knowledge of the facts, his reasoned arguments and objectivity, but also because of his phenomenal oratorical skills. In the years that followed, I made it a practice of heading to the same garden, whenever I could, in the hope of again savoring one of his lectures.

"Sons of Rome," he announced sternly one evening, as I approached the throng of mostly Roman students who had been waiting patiently for his arrival. He was tall, young in age, and had the demeanor of a very successful person. His garment was typically Athenian, consisting of a gray tunic, over which he had thrown a woolen *chiton* to protect him from the penetrating winter chill.

"If any of you have come this evening expecting to hear acclaim and words of praise for your empire, I am afraid you are in the wrong class. But, if your presence here is motivated by a desire to learn the truth regarding the past policies of Rome toward its conquered lands, its relations with Hellas, and of our two cities in particular, then I extend to you a cheerful and heartfelt welcome."

Total silence greeted his opening admonition. If there was disappointment, or even displeasure, on the part of the Roman students present, it did not become evident.

After the brief warning Andronikos began his talk. "My

Roman friends: Your presence in our city, which is universally accepted as a leading cultural center of the empire provides ample evidence, I believe, of the powerful bonds that link our two cities. It matters little any longer, that Rome once was the victor and Athens the vanquished. Our city stands today as a full partner of the imperial capital, a beacon of the arts, political theory, and philosophy, and the place where Rome's brightest sons, functionaries and even emperors visit to acquire the latest in human knowledge. Thousands of your youth attend our academies every year, and an even larger number of your citizens visit our city annually, attracted by our great monuments, the opportunity to celebrate the Olympic games, and to witness everything that is so unique and special here.

"I am aware that many of my brothers and sisters in the city, find it difficult to acknowledge that the unique cultural distinctions which Athens enjoys today are due to a large extent to the generosity of Rome.

"Athens could not have sustained its role as a leading cultural center of the empire, without the unselfish support of the imperial capital. It was the financial assistance from Rome that allowed our arts to flourish, and our academies to become the leading centers of learning that they are today.

"The search for knowledge has been of course a centuries-old tradition in Athens. A world famous academy had been in full operation here long before the first Roman legionnaires arrived to our shores. Established by our great philosopher Plato -- at this approximate spot where we now stand, I might add -- it has provided the model for several additional schools which have since been founded. But sadly, with the passage of time interest in philosophy and political theory has waned among Athenian youth. Some attribute this to the growth of Christianity, others to the fact that our city no longer enjoys the political and economic power and influence it once did. You, yourselves, can attest to this fact this evening; attending the lecture are but a few Athenian youth.

The bonds between our two cities, of which I spoke earlier, are nowhere more evident than in the constant stream of Roman visitors amongst us. The list includes many persons who have held the high office of emperor, including several leading contenders to the throne. Many of these visitors were so overtaken by the splendor of Athens, they became its benefactors, contributing funds for the erection of new structures or the repair of buildings damaged in earlier fighting.

"Emperors Pompey, Julius Caesar, Brutus, Cassius, and Marcus Antonius, spent extended periods of leisure time here during the early years of Roman rule. Marcus Antonius came on three different occasions, once with Cleopatra. Later emperors who made pilgrimages to our city included Tiberius, Caligula, Constantine, Domitian, and Trajan. Emperor Nero never visited Athens, although he spent a great deal of time touring Delphi, Olympia, and several other smaller towns and villages. He is remembered here mostly for his many antics, but also for declaring Hellas free of Roman rule. He did it, undoubtedly, in a moment of exuberant enthusiasm for Hellenic culture. Nero's freedom order was reversed, however, by his successor, Emperor Vespasian.

"Of all Roman visitors to Athens none has been more warmly welcomed, through the years, than the philhellene Emperor Hadrian. A regular presence for many years in our city, Hadrian enjoyed dressing and living like a native Athenian. He turned out to be also quite generous, directing that funds be spent for various beautification projects, and for providing the city with a modern water supply system. Numerous public buildings that Athenians enjoy today carry the insignia of the emperor. Hadrian was also instrumental for completing the largest temple ever built in Hellas, the high temple to Dias (Zeus) in Athens. Construction of this colossal temple, with its 104 columns, had begun six centuries earlier during the reign of Peisistratos, but it took a son of Rome to complete it. A grateful city declared Hadrian its honorary citizen, and decorated the *agora* with several of his statues on the day that the temple was sanctified.

"I understand that your countrymen refer to him as 'Graeculus," or the little Hellene, but here Hadrian is widely known as the "Great Philhellene." It was rightful for Athenians to embrace him with boundless love. Not since the time of Pericles, did the city look more festive and radiant than it did during his reign.

"So much, men, for the plusses of the Roman rule. Now for the minuses, of which there is a long list to choose from.

"Our relations with Rome would have been so much smoother, and our sources of friction far fewer, had your emperors shown greater respect for our political institutions. And also -- this is a big one -- had your legionnaires, generals, and even emperors not been... such notorious art thieves.

"No righteous person can deny that in the political arena Rome has been extremely generous toward Athens. During most years of Roman rule, we have enjoyed independence from day-to-day dictates of Roman functionaries, were allowed to draft our laws, and paid Rome only scant taxes.

We were also free of the requirement of stationing a Roman military garrison on our territory, which is a common practice in all cities of comparable size in the empire.

"But, this is the city of Solon and Cleon, remember? Of Klisthenes and Pericles! Democracy and human freedoms run in our veins. Although your emperors presumably are aware of this fact, they love to tinker with our democratic institutions, in the hope of bringing them more in line with Rome's autocratic rule. On orders from Rome, for instance, the role of our generals has been greatly enhanced. So has that of the Arios Pagos, which has evolved into the city's supreme political authority with responsibility for reviewing the laws enacted by our legislature. Our assembly, which for centuries has been the bulwark of our democratic government, has been reduced in importance by limits on how often it could meet.

"The independence and self-government granted to us by Rome, unfortunately, came to an end during the reign of Emperor Caracalla, when all persons living within the empire were ruled to be Roman citizens and subject to Roman law. The order was clearly designed to end our democratic government, and the political and economic freedoms enjoyed here."

"Master, is it not true that the only demand that Rome ever imposed on Athens, in return for these many freedoms was that it remain a loyal ally, a commitment which your city conveniently ignored on several occasions, or refused to fulfill outright? Similarly, is it not true that Rome always ended up forgiving Athens for these transgressions?"

The question by the Roman student momentarily startled Andronikos. Foreign students generally refrained from ask-king questions because of their difficulty in mastering the language spoken in Athens.

"Yes, young man," he replied, "you are correct on both counts. The Athenians, being a restless lot could not resist the temptation of opposing Rome when the opportunity presented itself. Repeatedly, through the years our city has sided with the enemies of Rome, only to find itself again and again on the losing side when Rome prevailed. Although Athens usually escaped punishment, because of Roman respect and admiration for our city and its history, on one occasion it paid dearly for defying the empire. I am referring, of course, to the time many years ago when king Mithradatos of Pontos challenged Rome's control of Asia Minor and Athens foolishly decided to join him. After soundly defeating the rebellious king, the Roman legions, under general Sulla, turned their ire upon Athens. An unprecedented orgy of burning and ravaging ensued, with Sulla personally encouraging his troops to kill, rape, and maim the hapless Athenians.

"During periods of Roman civil strife, too, when pretenders competed for the throne, Athens again would end up backing the wrong side. Thus, it sided with Pompey against Julius Caesar, and lost. It sided with Brutus and Cassius against Marcus Antonius, and lost. And it sided with Marcus Antonius against Octavian, and lost again.

"Repeatedly, when choosing sides, Athens made its decisions on sentiment rather than practical politics. Pompey, for instance, was supported in his contest against Julius Ceasar, because he had spent several years in our city studying under various philosophers. Brutus and Cassius, similarly drew a great deal of support from the people because they were perceived as defenders of liberty. Athenians were so enamored with them that they had their statues erected on the Acropolis. Marcus Antonius, like so many others whom Athens defied, decided against punishing the city, because of pride in his Athenian education; he brought gifts to Athens instead. Octavian similarly brought gifts, and substantial amounts of money to the city, despite the fact that it had rebelled against him. He directed, that the funds he donated be used for the construction of a large structure in the *agora*.

"As an interesting aside, whenever the Athenians survived a scare such as the ones mentioned, they would become extremely deferential toward the victor, erecting statues in his honor, and otherwise honoring him. When Julius Ceasar was assassinated, Athens erected statues honoring Brutus and Cassius. Marcus Antonius was honored even more so, when the city fathers in a moment of folly placed his statue and that of Cleopatra *inside* the Parthenon. In appreciation of the fact that Octavian did not destroy their city, Athenians erected a statue of him on horseback and placed it on the Propylaea, at the entrance to the Acropolis.

"So much, men, for the story of Rome's involvement in our political institutions, and for our city's fickle ways toward Rome. But, as I alluded to earlier, there is another far bigger resentment that we Athenians harbor against Rome. It concerns the theft, yes the wholesale theft by Romans, of all rank, of much of the art of classical Hellas. The theft was undertaken not only during the early years of war and conquest, when rules tend to be lax, but also in the following years. It was carried out with equal zeal by imperial civil functionaries, and military men of all ranks, including emperors.

"My former professor Evagoras would say that the main reason why the Romans occupied Hellas was to rob the land of its art treasures. I tend to agree with him. Look at the loot, for instance, in the form of statues, figurines, gold, and coins that the Roman troops presented to their leaders on their return to Rome following a military campaign in our lands. At the victory parade of Titus Flamininus for instance -- he was the general, you will recall, who after defeating the Macedonians promised Hellas that henceforth it would be free -- enormous amounts of gold, and works of arts were displayed. In fact, his victory parade lasted three full days with countless carts filled with gold, silver, and works of Hellenic art being paraded through the streets of Rome.

"At the victory parade of Pompey, too, numerous Hellenic gold statues were displayed, including mountains of gold, coins, and jewelry. Sulla, after overcoming Athenian resistance, helped himself to countless items of art, including some columns from the yet unfinished Temple of Dias (Zeus). This is the temple, you recall, that later Emperor Hadrian helped complete.

"The Roman looting of Hellenic art did not only occur as part of war. To this day, Roman officials are looting the territories under their control, and even cities and towns through which they happen to be traveling. The loot invariably finds its way to Rome, where it is often used to adorn palaces and public buildings, or is used as props for political campaigns.

"Every Roman emperor, it seems, who has ever visited Athens left with his hands full. The only exception was Hadrian. Not only did he not remove anything, but he added buildings for the beautification of the city and for the comfort of its citizens. Emperor Nero, too, was different. He raided the cities of Hellas relentlessly, but respected Athens.

"Karyatis?" Sophia interrupted.

"Something is beginning to trouble me. The theft of art from Hellas has been carried out for so very long, and by so many different peoples -- Persians, Romans, and others. Why suddenly the big fuss over the Elgin marbles?"

"You cannot be serious, Sophia! And, will you please stop referring to the Parthenon sculptures as the Elgin marbles? They don't belong to Elgin, they never did, so please do not call them that. They are the Parthenon sculptures, because they belong to the temple by that name on the Acropolis."

"All right, all right, I'll do that! But still my point, I think, is well taken. Why the big fuss, Karyatis? Will you please explain it to me? I am planning to discuss this issue with Edward, when he returns from Washington, and it would be helpful if I knew both sides of the debate."

"I'll be glad to, Sophia, but before taking up the subject with Edward, don't you want to hear first all of the gruesome details on the rape of Hellenic art?"

"You mean there is more?"

"Yes, during the Roman days alone, Hellenic art was ravaged on three other occasions, once when that bloodthirsty Roman general Sulla entered Athens, and twice afterwards by barbarian invaders from the north known as the Goths."

"I'm listening."

You must recall Andronikos' comment, earlier, that the Athenians wishing to be free of Roman rule missed no opportunity to betray Rome. Athens took up arms against the imperial capital repeatedly by siding with its enemies, only to find itself at the end of the war on the side of the defeated. But luckily, Athens escaped punishment for these indiscretions, when Rome would choose to forgive the city out of respect for its past glory and gifts to world culture and civilization.

There was one major exception to this cycle of betrayal and forgiveness, however. When Athens elected to ally herself with the young and gifted King Mithradatos of Pontos, who had rebelled against Rome, the results turned catastrophic. General Sulla, one of the more ruthless tyrants ever to run the empire, after defeating the Pontian king and forcing him to sue for peace, turned his ire on Athens. The tragedy that followed was greater than the one the city had endured centuries earlier in the hands of the Persians. On entering Athens, Sulla's legionnaires raped, killed, plundered, and burnt, for days on end.

I think I'll let Kleodimos fill in the details. He was one of a handful of the Athenian defenders who hid in my temple after Sulla's troops had marched into the city. He managed somehow to survive the siege, and also the slaughter that followed. In later years after serving the city in a variety of important posts, Kleodimos would return to his former hideout with his two granddaughters, Myra and Cleio, to recite for them the events of what had been undoubtedly one of the darkest moments in Athenian history.

"We had been under Roman rule for over half a century," I remember him reminiscing one afternoon, as if trying to rationalize for the two young girls the reasons for the Athenian rebellion. "They were the conquerors and masters; we, the defeated and their servants. It was only natural for us to want to take up arms against Rome, whenever the opportunity arose."

Sitting near the spot where he had taken refuge from Sulla's troops many years earlier, he looked unlike the brave but frightened adolescent I remembered watching in horror while his beloved Athens was being ravaged by foreign troops.

"From the outset, King Mithradatos had many followers in Athens. People admired his youth, his skill in battle and ability to inflict the kind of punishment upon the Romans that they had imposed on others (Corinth, for instance). Leading the pro-Mithradatos faction in Athens was Athenion, a philosopher, whose speeches on the Arios Pagos did much to inflame and rekindle the Hellenic hatred toward Rome. Athens responded by formally declaring itself an ally of the Pontian king, and in a moment of exuberant optimism, even agreed to the stationing of several thousand of the king's troops on its territory. When the troops arrived, the fate of Athens as an enemy of Rome had been sealed.

"It did not take long for Sulla, after defeating the Pontian ruler and forcing him to surrender, to appear before the walls of our city".

"Where were you at the time mega pater," I recall the older of the girls ask. "Were you in this very spot?"

"No! I was actually at the other end of the city, Myra. I was a mere *hoplite* then, responsible with a dozen or so other men for defending the gate on the Long Wall, through which passed the road that led to the temple at Sounion. I would be lying to you, of course, if I denied being scared at the sight of the Roman legions. I had never seen so many armed men and vehicles of war as had been lined up outside our walls that evening.

"Soon we heard that Sulla had asked permission to enter our city, but that he had been refused by general Aristion, our ruler at the time. Even though Aristion was not particularly popular with the people of Athens, there was wide support for his decision to keep Sulla out. We were young and defiant, perhaps even a bit foolish, but we believed deeply in the cause of defending our city. The presence of the Pontian forces in the port of Piraeus gave us an added sense of confidence.

"Unfortunately, there was a major drawback in the military situation which we, as plain *hoplite*s, were not aware of. The wall linking Athens with Piraeus, on which both our cities depended for communications and resupply had fallen in disrepair, making the formation of a unified front against the enemy impossible. It did not take long for Sulla to recognize this shortcoming in our defenses, and the opportunity it afforded him to strike our two cities, one at a time. He left a small force outside Athens to ensure that no food or livestock could enter the city and marched his legions on Piraeus.

"Attacking the port city turned out a lot more difficult, however. Piraeus was protected by powerful fortifications, and to breach them Sulla required high catapults which he did not possess. Fortunately for him, but sadly for us, there was plenty of timber in the area and boulders for that purpose. On his orders, all trees lining the route to the famous Academy of Plato were cut to provide the required timber, and long sections of the wall between Athens and Piraeus were demolished to provide the stones and rubble required to build the huge platforms on which to mount the catapults. When the machines were finally ready and in place he launched his attack.

"His forces were repulsed but attacked again without success. Frustrated, Sulla attempted to bypass the fortifications by excavating tunnels underneath them. But the men digging the tunnels soon reported encountering solid rock, that could not be penetrated.

"In Athens we would hear with great pride of the resistance against Sulla's legions by our brother Hellenes in Piraeus. But these successes were of no help to us and our own escalating problem -- which was hunger. An extremely tight Roman blockade had made it impossible for food or livestock to find its way into the city. Hunger was so widespread that anything growing, and even animals, were used for food.

"Attacked savagely by Sulla's war machines the defenders of Piraeus eventually gave up. Sulla entered the city triumphantly and promptly ordered that it be destroyed. After burning for several days, the port facilities, fortifications, and the city itself of Piraeus ceased to exist.

"Our turn was next. When the Roman tyrant finally launched his attack on our city, he used every healthy legionnaire and war machine under his command.

"Large boulders fired by the Roman catapults soon began hitting our walls, with several boulders missing the walls and landing in the center of the *agora*. The effect was devastating. They took down not only sections of the wall but also individual residences, *stoas*, monuments, and public buildings. Exhausted by the continuous pounding and anxious for any form of nourishment, we began to weaken.

"Still, Sulla never succeeded in breaking our wall by force. He entered the city only after overhearing some men discuss the wall's weakness in the area of the Heptachalcum. Visiting the place at nighttime. he confirmed that indeed the wall was assailable at that point. He struck there the next morning with such violence that within hours his men were able to enter the city. Carnage followed, with Sulla himself urging his troops to rape, kill, and destroy everyone and everything Athenian. Exhausted by hunger and the deprivations of the siege, the city residents were unable to resist or even escape. Thousands were slain and numerous others committed suicide, rather than fall victim to the attacking troops. As for Sulla, after resisting all pleas to end the slaughter claiming that he had come to teach the Athenians obedience, he relented eventually and ordered the killing to stop. Ironically, when he issued his order he praised classical Hellas, declaring that he forgave the living for the sake of the dead."

"What about you, mega pater? Where were you when his order was announced?"

"It did not affect me or many other Athenian fighters. Several hundred of us had taken refuge right here on the Acropolis, when it had become clear that Sulla and his men were about to enter the city. To our good fortune, Sulla decided to wait us out rather than attack right away. Good that he did, because without food and even water we could not have lasted long. We surrendered once the killing in the city stopped. Aristion and some of our officers lost their lives, on orders of Sulla; all others, including your mega pater were let go."

"That Sulla, must have been a very evil person."

"The worse kind! But do you, girls, want to hear something very strange? Years later, when he was asked what his greatest accomplishment in life was, he claimed that saving Athens from destruction was. By that he meant, I am sure, not destroying Athens, the way he had ruined Piraeus.

"The damage to our city was grievous. I remember the shock that I experienced when I visited the *agora,* after the Roman troops withdrew. Public buildings, stoas, stalls, and nearly all houses had been razed to the ground by the angry troops.

"Sulla systematically looted the country of anything that appealed to him during his stay in Hellas. Nothing escaped his enormous hunger: paintings, marble statues, busts, or columns from temples. If he liked something he would simply ship it to Rome. Sulla also helped himself to huge amounts of gold and silver from the treasury of the Parthenon, and also from Olympia, Delphi, and Epidauros. He also removed hundreds of military shields that had been stored by the Athenian authorities in the Stoa of Zeus Eleutherios. When he finally returned to Rome at the end of his campaign, his victory parade lasted several days, with scores of chariots drawn through the streets of the capital city laden with the loot from Hellas."

In the years following Sulla, Sophia, the fortunes of Athens became more closely bound to the empire than ever before. When the empire prospered, Athens prospered also. But when the empire was threatened from beyond its borders, Athens similarly was threatened. Thus, it was Hellas and Athens that paid a high price when the Goths and later the

Visigoths broke through the Roman defenses and invaded the empire.

The Goth and Visigoth invasions occurred during a period of great personal upheaval for me -- when my own survival, Sophia, had become my principal preoccupation. Looking back I had very good reasons to be concerned. Christianity was expanding, the few Athenians who were still adhering to the Olympian faith were being persecuted, and numerous temples and sanctuaries throughout the city were either being torn down or converted into Christian churches. Visitors to the Acropolis would occasionally mention stories of individual statues being crushed into boulders, or converted into powder for use in construction. My fright had become so great that for a while, I stopped caring about the city itself. It made little difference to me any longer whether Romans, Goths, or Visigoths ruled what formerly was Hellas.

I did not learn the circumstances of the two invasions until much later, Sophia, from a Byzantine scholar whose name I believe was Michael. The talk around town was that Michael was the tutor of a Byzantine prince, whom he had escorted to Athens on an orientation and study mission.

"The Goths' appearance in Athens," I recall him telling the young prince, "occurred during a period that the Roman empire was clearly in decline. Power was in the hands of the army, with one emperor replacing another amid chaos and the lack of the rule of law. Wars between rival emperors were common place and crime was rampant.

"The Goths who were the strongest of the German tribes then living north of the Danube river, sensed in the prevailing

Roman disarray an opportunity for conquest. Moving on two fronts, one on land through the Balkans, the other by sea through the Bosporus, plundering and ravaging on the way, they appeared suddenly before the walls of Athens. Finding the city empty (its population had conveniently departed for fear of being slaughtered) the Goths went on a savage rampage. Few art treasures were left untouched, and the entire *agora* was totally devastated.

"Fortunately, as quickly as the Goths had arrived they also departed, when a small force of Athenians under the command of Dexippos ambushed some of their troops north of the city. Dexippos became an instant celebrity after his victory and was honored greatly. Later, he was even crowned king.

"The Visigoth invasion many years later was again the result of Rome's inability to protect its northern frontiers. Threatened by Huns moving into central Europe, the Visigoths under King Alaric broke through the Roman defenses and advanced south. Devastation followed, as the victorious invaders raided one Hellenic city after another.

"King Alaric never entered Athens, however. It was said, that on arriving before the walls of the city he saw the images of Goddess Athena and of Achilles, fully-armed, protecting the ramparts. He became so frightened by the sight that he chose not to take the city by force. On hearing the news, the authorities invited him into the city, and received him with great honors; even presented him with numerous gifts. Alaric took a short walk through the *agora,* visited the local baths, and departed leaving everything intact. But he more than made up for his kindness to Athens by ravaging later several cities in the Peloponnese, especially, Corinth, and Argos.

After completing the plunder and pillage of the Hellenic countryside, Alaric led his men north, their wagons piled high with the loot. Eventually, he entered Rome which he proceeded to plunder royally before departing again en route to Spain."

"Bet, you were scared through it all, Karyatis."

"It was scary at times! Not knowing who these people were and whether they intended to stay.

"I have one last piece on the Roman years, Sophia, if you still have time. It concerns Emperor Nero, undoubtedly the most unstable and cruel person ever to occupy the Imperial throne."

"I recall the story of him lounging with friends and enjoying a theatrical performance, while his capital city of Rome was burning."

"It is a true story. The crew of an Athenian merchant ship, that happened to be visiting Rome at that time witnessed the event. The fire raged for an entire week, and Nero's only reaction was to enjoy life and blame it all on the Christians.

"No normal person, of course, would behave that way. What can one say? Nero was not normal; he was a vicious, cruel man. He was even cruel to the officials in his immediate circle. There are stories about scores of his counselors and other servants losing their lives as a result of palace intrigues, which he personally instigated."

Most of what I know of Nero, Sophia, is based on conversations that I overheard by visitors to my temple, during the time when the emperor was in Hellas. He never made it to

Athens, the way other emperors did. Rumors had it that after he had his own mother killed, he did not wish to visit Athens for fear that the gods might punish him.

"He murdered his own mother?"

"He sure, did!"

There are rumors that he put to death also his wife Octavia. Still, there was one redeeming value about him. At the end of his reign, when rebellious troops reached his palace, and he was informed that the Roman Senate had ordered his death, he committed suicide rather than put up a fight.

According to the talk of town at that time, the great fire of Rome presented Nero with the unique opportunity to rebuild his capital city. His first act, after the fire, was to build for himself a huge new palace, which he appropriately named the "Golden House." The palace was devoid, of course, of art treasures, which might explain his decision to visit Hellas soon thereafter.

Nero literally emptied Delphi of all art, removing hundreds of statues and treasures of all kinds, including the famed statue of Hydra that had been erected by grateful Hellenes in appreciation of the semi-goddess' help in destroying the Persian fleet outside Pelion. The city of Olympia similarly fell victim to Nero's enormous appetite for art. Its most notable items ended up decorating the "Golden House." Among them was a sculpture of Odysseus of Trojan War fame, and also life size statues of Zeus and Dionysos.

The theft of art was not the emperor's only reason for visiting Hellas. Nero was a frustrated poet and composer. In Rome, he claimed, his talents were not being appreciated so he chose Hellas as the venue for his artistic work. For several months he toured the Hellenic countryside acting at performances, and competing at festivals as a musician and poet. Of course he "won" all contests which he entered. In Olympia he even participated in the Olympic games, "winning" a chariot race even though he fell off his chariot in the process. When news of his antics reached Rome, he became the subject of numerous jokes, especially when he began insisting that he be accorded the honors of an Olympic champion.

There isn't really much more to say about him, Sophia. Everyone who came in contact with him said that Nero loved Hellas with all his heart, but Hellas could have done without him. Even his so-called gift, when he granted Hellas freedom from Roman rule, proved to be fake. It was promptly reversed by his successor.

"Are we done with the Roman period, Karyatis?"

"Yes."

"I'd better be going, then."

"So soon?"

"I am afraid I have to.

"On my way to the spa this morning, I passed a jewelry consignment shop. In its window display there was a set of earrings that looked very much like a pair that my mother was wearing in my last photo of her. It was early morning and the store was closed, but it should be open now. I've got to have these earrings!

"Have I ever told you of my Mum? I lost her and my Dad, too, in a fire while I was still quite young. But I remember her as the sweetest, most thoughtful woman anyone could know. I don't remember much of Dad, though. He was the manager of a pub in Leeds where we lived, but his hours were such that he could spend only very little time with me."

"I am sorry to hear, Sophia, that you too have met a lot of pain and disappointment in life. By the way, how is the portrait coming along?"

"Making good progress."

"Will I get a chance to see it, when it is finished? I am curious to see what I look like."

"You know that you are beautiful, Karyatis. Why do you even ask?

"Forgot to mention. I may not be coming in for a couple of days. With the Christmas holidays approaching, there is a great deal that I need to take care of. I will be back, though, as soon as I can. I promise."

"You will not forget me?"

"No, I won't!"

VI

INTERLUDE

Sophia's comment to the Caryatid, that Christmas preparations would prevent her from returning the next morning, was a cover story. With Edward still in Washington, preoccupied with his Byzantine coins, there was really little that she needed to do to prepare for the holiday. But having spent three full days with her, listening to her exhaustive recollections of fact and tale, Sophia suddenly felt the need to be alone.

Alone, to think and contemplate the many issues that her newly found friend had raised, and their relevance to her own life as an artist, a friend of Edward, and even a Briton. When she had asked the Caryatid earlier to share her life's story with her, she had no idea of the black hole she was about to be drawn into. For one, the statue's recollections had suddenly reawakened her desire to learn all she could of her own prior life, a life she was certain had involved her in some capacity on the Acropolis in Athens.

Once, during the statue's narrative, Sophia had felt such attachment to the events being described, it nearly convinced her that somehow she had been a part of them when they occurred. It also confirmed her earlier suspicion, that her prior life in some way had been linked with the fortunes of Athena, the long-since forgotten goddess of the Hellenes.

Far more important, however, the Caryatid's recollections had been instrumental in arousing Sophia's curiosity about the various causes that the statue was espousing. Was it fair she found herself wondering for the British Museum to keep the Parthenon sculptures -- the statue's insistence that she refer to them as Parthenon sculptures, rather than Elgin marbles, had begun to take hold -- rather than return them to Athens whence they had come from and where they belonged? Was it fair for any museum to display art that had been acquired under questionable circumstances, and which did not legally belong to it? Was this an issue in which she wanted to become involved?

Sophia found two messages on her answering machine when she entered her studio. The first was from a fellow artist announcing the scheduling of a private showing of "China Unearthed," a widely anticipated show on art treasures recently discovered in China. Would Sophia be interested in attending, she inquired. The second message was from Edward. He had been under the weather for most of the day in windy and cold Washington and had decided to remain in bed."Talk to you in the morning," he added.

She was not troubled by the curt message. Edward was always brief and business-like on the phone, the result of his many daily contacts with students and research assistants at the university, where time is at a premium.

Her studio was frigid as usual, with a leaky kitchen window dissipating whatever little warmth was coming through the heating system. Instinctively she reached for the thermostat, and despite her landlord's repeated warnings that energy be conserved, she turned the switch to the maximum setting. With Edward still in Washington, and snow covered slippery streets outside, this was definitely a stay-at-home evening and she intended to make the most of it in terms of personal comfort.

Bundled in a wool blanket, a cup of steaming tea and a box of biscuits on a stand in front of her, she reached for the small book that had caught her attention while browsing earlier that day in the Museum's book store. Her original intent in visiting the store had been to find a book dealing with the life of her new friend the Caryatid, or Karyatis as she preferred to be called. She wanted to learn all she could about her; how she had been removed from the Acropolis, her arrival in London, and her whereabouts before finally being turned over to the British Museum. She preferred to hear it all from a neutral objective source, not that she did not believe the Caryatid's version. But the Hellenic statue was so incensed with her involuntary confinement in London, that she had a tendency to exaggerate, perhaps even fib a bit to prove her point. Like her earlier story that King Alaric of the Visigoths decided not to attack Athens, because he saw the images of Goddess Athena and of Achilles on the ramparts of the city walls! Imagine that!

Unable to locate a book or other publication that dealt

exclusively with the story of the Caryatid, Sophia turned her attention next to the various accounts displayed on the store's shelves dealing with the acquisition by the British Museum of the Parthenon sculptures. One of them seemed especially informative. "I think, I'll take this one," she told the clerk, "and please have it wrapped." The last thing she needed was for the Caryatid to notice the book's title, and then launch on yet another tirade on the author lack of judgment for referring to the Parthenon sculptures as the Elgin marbles.

Competing for Sophia's attention on the stand next to her was a second book; the one she had purchased earlier that month at a bookstore on Oxford Street, as a gift for a friend in the arts community. It took only a few minutes before she felt captivated by its contents. Here was a book dealing with the very story that the Caryatid had been narrating: the pillage of Hellenic art through the ages, by Persians, Roman emperors, and even Renaissance noblemen. Four hours later, after devouring every page of the work, including an engaging description of how the Aegean treasures at the Louvre had been retrieved from their centuries-old resting places and moved to Paris, Sophia laid the book aside.

She had visited the Louvre, of course, on several occasions and had admired, examined and even sketched the leading Hellenic treasures there. Praxiteles' masterpiece, known the world over as the Aphrodite of Melos, and the Winged Victory of Samothrace, were not only exceptional works of art but to an artist like her the ultimate in human expression. Odd as it sounded, she had never questioned why these statues happened to be in Paris and not in Athens. It was the question that the Caryatid was now asking about herself.

But the world's museums are full of works of art that in earlier times had belonged to someone else, Sophia pondered, while preparing for bed. Must all of them be returned to their places of origin? If not all, which ones? Where would one draw the line? And how would one know today who the rightful owner of a given work of art is, especially for art removed from empires or peoples long gone?

Edward's call the following morning lasted a lot longer than usual. The bed rest and a good night's sleep seemed to have rejuvenated him. He peppered Sophia with questions about the London art scene, progress on her painting, news of mutual friends, including one concerning her social life that made her feel rather unsettled.

"No, Edward," she answered firmly, "my only companion last evening was a book on the art of Hellas, and how it was devoured through the years by invaders, wars, etc."

"You mean by Romans, crusaders, that sort of a thing?"

"Yes, and also our own Lord Elgin."

"Of course.

"Actually, Sophia, there was enough marble statuary in classical Hellas to go around for everyone," he answered sort of facetiously. "Archaeologists tell us that at about the time of Christ there were more marble statues than people in that corner of the world".

"Hardly an excuse, though, for the kind of stealing and

plundering that followed," she answered pointedly.

Edward suddenly realized that his clumsy joke, and its implication that there had been plenty of marble statues in Hellas for everyone to steal with impunity, had not gone well with Sophia. It had been just a thoughtless quip. How was he to know that she was in the mood for a serious discussion this early in the morning?

He tried to make amends. "Of course not. And as you know by now, having read the book, factors other than aesthetic impulses were behind most such plundering. Sulla, for instance, looted the art of Athens and all of Hellas in order to produce the largest triumphal procession in Roman history, not because he appreciated the beauty of the art."

"It's a fascinating subject and one which I would like us to discuss when you return home. In the meantime, I'll do some more reading on it."

"Good idea, Sophia."

"On a different subject, Edward," she continued. "What are your thoughts about the fundraiser that the University Club will be sponsoring early next spring? Will you be again a sponsor? It is scheduled for March 20th, and I have a scheduling conflict on that evening. Would you mind if I skip the fundraiser? It's Elizabeth Stokes' birthday, and a group of us girls are organizing a birthday party for her."

"No problem Sophia. You know that I don't really enjoy these events. I'll just make a brief appearance that evening, long enough to appease the University's Chancellor, and then depart."

VII

MOTHER OF EMPRESSES

"Great news, Karyatis," whispered Sophia playfully, as soon as she made eye contact with her. "Edward showed up at my doorstep on Christmas Eve. He could not bear it, he said, being alone in Washington during the holidays, so at a moment's notice he caught a flight back to London. It was great being with him again."

"I could tell, Sophia, as soon as you entered the building this morning, that something very special had happened during the days that you were gone. It is written all over you; you look simply radiant, today.

"I also love those new earrings that you are wearing and the silver pin," she added, as if in an afterthought.

"Thank you my friend, you are so very kind. The pin is a gift from Edward. As for the earrings, they were still at the store when I got there the other evening, so I grabbed them; didn't even quibble over their price."

"With all these joyful happenings in your life, I wonder

young lady whether you'll really be up to -- listening, I mean more of my story."

"Of course I want to," Sophia replied with emphasis. "Why do you think I ventured out into the cold this morning? Your story, Karyatis, challenges me in more ways than you know."

"Challenges you? I am not sure that I understand!"

"I'll have to explain it to you at another time."

"All right then, since you insist, we might as well get started."

I hope you recall, Sophia, the philosopher Andronikos telling us that for a while Athens fared well under Roman rule. But the invasions by the Goth and Visigoth barbarian tribes, and the closing by Emperor Justinian of the academies for which Athens was famous, landed such major blows to the city that it was unable to recover. With its temples already converted to Christian *ecclesies,* and its works of art stolen or destroyed by enemy forces and religious fanatics, Athens could no longer claim to be a "center of culture," or the "museum of antiquity," titles it held for hundreds of years.

"Emperor Justinian, Karyatis, the one who built the famed Haghia Sophia Cathedral in Constantinople, ordered the closing of the academies of Athens? Why on earth did he do such a thing?"

"Religious fanaticism, Sophia. As a devout Christian he wanted to eradicate the last vestiges in the faith of the Olympian gods, which he believed drew its strength from the universities and the study of philosophy."

"Very strange!"

After the closing of the academies most of their professors and academics sought refuge in Persia. A few stubbornly refused to leave, however. "Whatever few days I have left in my life," I recall one of them saying, "I intend to spend them here in the city of Socrates and Plato." He spent his last years roaming the city, and also the Acropolis, a sad and dejected man, complaining of the "horrors" that Emperor Justinian had inflicted upon his beloved Athens.

"What horrors?" I heard a tall brawny man ask one evening, as he and two companions walked past my temple at the conclusion of the Vesper services in the Church of Panaghia Athiniotissa. "I swear," he added, "I don't know what you fellows are talking about!"

"Don't be angry at us, Eukrates," answered one of his companions."The word in the city is that Justinian hates Athens, and is determined to thrash it into oblivion."

"Nonsense" replied Eukrates contemptuously. "Absolute and total nonsense!

"Why do you fellows even bother listening to rumors spread by pagans, who still believe that gods actually reside on Mount Olympus? Emperor Justinian has bestowed upon our city nothing but favors and goodwill. He has given us autonomy from the capital city of Thebes, and has helped us rebuild our walls as a protection against barbarian invasions. Our city's only obligation toward Byzantium is to present each new emperor and empress with a wreath of gold, symbolic of the city's loyalty to them.

I strained to listen. It was rare those days to hear laudatory comments in Athens about the emperor. Eukrates, I soon learned had just returned from Constantinople where he and hundreds of other masons had participated in the construction of the Great Church of Haghia Sophia, the emperor's great design.

"Don't listen to those ugly rumors," Eukrates repeated. "Justinian is a gifted and tireless leader, who along with his very able wife, the Empress Theodora, is building an enormous empire to take the place of what was once Rome. Not just any empire though, but one that is Christian Orthodox in faith and Hellenic in spirit. We, as Orthodox Christians and descendents of Pericles and Plato should be especially proud of this fact.

"It is true," he continued, "that the emperor closed our academies, and has imposed Christianity on those of our citizens who still believe in the pagan gods. Can you really blame him for that? For far too long, Athens has remained faithful to Mount Olympus, even after Christianity had been accepted as the official religion in the rest of Hellas, and much of the Mediterranean region."

"But why did Justinian have to destroy so many of our old temples in the process," demanded one of the men. "They were such lovely structures, symbolic of our old faith. The sanctuary of Dionysos, for instance, was turned into rubble; nothing remains any longer. As for the academies for which Athens was world famous, not only did the emperor shut them down, but he also suspended the salaries of their professors. Many have since gone to Persia. Athens is being drained of its brainpower and sliding into darkness."

"It was going to happen sooner or later," Eukrates explained. "Athens is no longer the center of the cosmos that it once was; it is not even the leading city of Hellas. Constantinople is where the heart of the world beats. Unfortunately, in the Imperial capital there is a lot of resentment toward our city and its long and glorious past. The resentment, as you know, is mutual. Everyone I have spoken to in Athens resents Constantinople's transformation, from a small village to an Imperial capital and the center of the arts."

"It all happened at our expense, Eukrates! A myriad of our statues and other art treasures that formerly graced our city are now in Byzantium. Of those that remained behind, many were shipped to Constantinople to provide the marble for the construction of Justinian's Great Church."

"True, along with marble from numerous other cities of Hellas, and also from Rome and Ephesus. The emperor wished the new church to be the Mother Church of the entire empire -- not of Constantinople alone -- and emphasized this point by including construction materials from a variety of sources.

"After fires had ravaged the earlier structure of Haghia Sophia, Justinian conceived this grandiose project of rebuilding the church on a much larger scale. Construction lasted five years, and I was among the hundreds of workers fortunate enough to have participated, often working under the direct supervision of the emperor himself. With the basic structure in place, Justinian is sparing now no expense in furnishing the Great Church with the finest marble, mosaics, precious stones, and painted icons."

"During your travels elsewhere in the empire, Eukrates, what did you find to be the prevailing feelings for our city? What do people think of us now?"

"Do you really wish to hear the truth?"

"Yes."

"Only our memory remains; at most, we are considered the remnants of a venerable old city."

"Sadly, Sophia, what Eukrates mentioned was true. Occupying an out-of-the way and insignificant corner of the empire, and deprived of any political and cultural importance, Athens remained a "has been" city throughout the Byzantine years. In fact, had it not been for the fact that three Athenian women served as empresses in Constantinople, and for visits to our city by two Byzantine emperors, Athens would not have been heard from for centuries."

"Athens, the city that illuminated the world had been relegated to a mere insignificant dot on the map?"

"Yes, which explains, Sophia, why Athens took such great pride whenever one of its daughters would ascend the throne of Constantinople. For the record, no Athenian man was ever crowned emperor during Byzantium's long history."

"I, along with everyone else, was very proud of these women. As Athenians gathered to talk and gossip, the subject would invariably turn to their sister in Constantinople, the power that she was yielding and her actions toward her native city, which as a rule were always very positive.

"I know the life histories of these three women, Sophia, by heart, having heard them dozens of times by visitors on the Acropolis or whenever I would venture into the city below."

"Was the famed Empress Theodora, wife of Justinian, one of them?"

"No, she was not. She hailed from the island of Cyprus, I

believe. Theodora was definitely not an Athenian."

The first Athenian woman to ascend the Byzantine throne, Sophia, was a beautiful maiden by the name of Athenais, the daughter of the philosopher Leontios. Even though not a Christian herself, she became the bride of Emperor Theodosios. You remember him! He was the one who forced Christianity upon the people of Hellas, and had issued those repulsive orders prohibiting the use of temples for honoring the Olympian gods. He was a real Christian zealot! The worst kind!

After converting to Christianity, Athenais took on the name of Evdokia and joined her husband in his senseless war against the faith of her ancestors. But she never forgot her Athenian roots. Repeatedly, she influenced the emperor to dispense favors on the city, including the granting of a very generous form of self-government and tax-free status.

Anxious to learn more of her new religion, Evdokia traveled to Jerusalem where she remained for an entire year, returning home with numerous Christian relics. But soon she fell from her husband's favor, probably due to the machinations of his sister, Pulcheria. Evdokia was exiled from Constantinople, and spent her remaining years in sadness; a lonely nun in a convent in Jerusalem.

Irene, the second Athenian woman to wear the Byzantine crown, served as empress not only while her husband was emperor, but also on her own right when she became the regent for her son.

Like Evdokia before her, Irene had the looks and the brains befitting an empress. She was only seventeen and living as an orphan in Athens when Emperor Constantine, the Fifth, selected her to be the bride of his son, Leon. She was brought to the Imperial capital where she married Leon, and when Constantine died, she was crowned empress.

When Irene arrived in Constantinople the city was under the influence of the iconoclasts, with the emperor and his son (her husband) continuing the iconoclast policies of their predecessors. Clergy and lay persons who resisted their orders were persecuted, and any remaining icons or other religious images still in homes, churches, or public buildings were ordered destroyed.

As an Athenian, Irene was a lover of images but was forced to renounce their use in order to marry Leon. Later, however, when Emperor Constantine and her own husband Emperor Leon died, and she came to power, she convened a council of bishops that branded iconoclasm a heresy, thus allowing the reintroduction of icons into churches. As we shall see later, the debate over icon worship did not end there.

Irene had an enormous appetite for power. When her husband died , she had herself appointed regent for her underage son Constantine, in practice becoming the sole ruler of the empire. But later, when Constantine grew into manhood and attempted to exercise the power that was legally his, she had him blinded."

"She blinded her own son?"

"Yes!"

Irene paid dearly for her crime. A revolution by Nikiforos Logothetis sent her packing into exile, on the island of Lesvos. The act must have come as a complete surprise to her. Days only prior to being exiled, Irene had been in the midst of marriage negotiations with Charlemagne, the crowned head of the Holy Roman Empire. Had a union of the two emperors materialized, it would in effect have reunited East and West for the first time after five hundred years.

Which brings me to Theano, a distant relative of Irene and the third Athenian woman to rule as empress. Theano was a married woman living in Athens with her husband, when Emperor Nikiforos Logothetis identified her as a prospective bride for his son, Stavrakos. She was made to divorce her husband and on orders of the emperor was brought to Constantinople, where amid great splendor she married the future emperor. The marriage proved short-lived. Stavrakos died not long after ascending the throne, and Theano ended her life in a convent.

“To the world of art, Karyatis, the iconoclast period was a tragedy. Thousands of works of Byzantine and Hellenic art, unequaled in beauty and historical significance, were destroyed for no good reason.”

"The iconoclast movement, Sophia, was only one of several religious conflicts that tormented Byzantium. Every few years or so it seemed, another religious dispute would erupt in the Imperial capital, causing unending arguments and divisions."

“In Athens, I recall it said once," Sophia interrupted, "during the Golden Age of Pericles, people would debate politics and democracy, or reflect on the latest plays by Euripides or Aristophanes, as a daily routine. But in Constantinople, the leading subject of discussion, in fact the only serious subject of concern was religion and the Christian dogma.”

"The Byzantines had great difficulty, Sophia, comprehending their new faith, especially the divinity of Christ and the concept of the Holy Trinity. They would debate forever the nature of Christ, and whether Father and Son are of the same essence. Major heresies would result whenever agreement on such issues could not be reached.

"Personally, I had little interest in all that Christian infighting. I did enjoy, however, hearing that many Christians were frustrated trying to understand their new God, that there was confusion over the divinity of Christ, and the veneration that Christians should offer to his Mother Mary. Our Olympic gods were so much simpler; one knew precisely what each one of them stood for.

"Was Athens directly affected by the iconoclast movement?"

"More so than other cities. Athens was violently opposed to the removal of icons from its churches. Once it even launched a naval campaign against Byzantium, to remove the iconoclast emperor from his throne and have him replaced with a pro-icon man. The candidate, incidentally, was an Athenian named Kosmas whose only claim to fame was his love for icons."

"You mean, small, unimportant Athens actually launched a naval campaign against all-powerful Constantinople? Its leaders could not have been serious!"

"It turned out, of course, into a true fiasco."

The leader of the anti-iconoclast movement in Athens, Sophia, and probably of all of Hellas, was Bishop Gregorios, a hierarch of flawless religious credentials, famed for his stalwart defense of the Orthodox faith. Gregorios had connections at the highest levels of the Church, throughout the Orthodox East, and despite his opposition to the iconoclast policies of the emperor, his advice and counsel was sought out regularly by the state and church authorities in the Imperial capital.

Gregorios enjoyed enormous popularity in Athens and huge crowds would gather whenever he spoke. With no church large enough to accommodate his followers, many of his religious services were held outdoors on the Acropolis. In a city starved for intellectual nourishment, Bishop Gregorios was like a breath of fresh air, and his sermons became the talk of town.

I could always tell, Sophia, whenever Gregorios was scheduled to address his flock on an important matter. Hours earlier, every open space between my temple and the Parthenon, which served at that time as the Bishop's own Cathedral, would be filled to capacity. On one particular evening, even I could tell that the address would be crucial, for Gregorios had just returned from Constantinople.

"Beloved brothers and sisters in Christ," were his opening words to the overflow crowd. "I bring somber news from the Imperial capital. Once again our faith is being tested. It is being challenged by the same group of fanatics whom the church years ago had condemned as heretics.

"We have no right, they allege, to venerate our God or to keep images of Christ and of his Mother the *Theotokos* in our homes. Neither may we decorate our churches with images depicting our saints, the prophets or evangelists.

"When we do so, they say, we are worshipping idols.

"Such rubbish! Such nonsense! I ask you: how can the image of Christ on the Cross be considered an idol?

"Athenians, I beseech you. I implore every one of you. Pay no heed to the voices of heresy. Do not allow these apostates to steer you away from the one true faith. They are distorting the reason icons and other religious images occupy such an important part in our lives, our homes and in our churches.

"The iconoclast movement," he reminded his assembled audience, "is not new. It has been around for a great many years. It was defeated and condemned as a heresy, but it refuses to give up. It continues to torment our people.

"The movement first raised its ugly head nearly a hundred years ago, when the misguided Emperor Leon, influenced by Muslims and Jews, decreed that all religious images and representations of the human form are idols. On his order, icons in private homes, churches, monasteries, and in public buildings were destroyed. Leon himself set the example by directing that the large gold icon of Christ, which for centuries adorned the bronze door of the Imperial palace, be removed and destroyed. The emperor's iconoclast anger was not limited to painted icons only. Books illustrating the life of Christ were similarly burned or destroyed, and mosaics were washed over with asbestos.

"From the very outset our city resisted this outrage. Who can forget those gallant Athenian men who along with several hundred other Hellenes sailed to the Bosporus not long ago in the hope of overturning the blasphemous policy? Yes, it was a proud fleet that set sail toward Constantinople; the secret hopes of all Christianity sailed with it. But it was not meant to be. Our fleet was brutally attacked by superior forces. After its defeat, the Athenian Kosmas, whom we had hoped to install as the next Byzantine emperor, was arrested and summarily executed.

"Emperor Leon learned nothing from this tragedy. If anything, he felt strengthened by it. He issued decrees ordering even stricter enforcement of his iconoclast policies, while dispatching hordes of soldiers to comb the Byzantine countryside in search of those violating his orders. Monasteries were destroyed, and monks were put to death, tortured or banished. Not even relics survived his frenzy, with iconoclast zealots breaking shrines open, and burning the remains of the saints buried inside. When Patriarch Germanos protested these actions, the emperor had him deposed. Our own Church in Hellas paid a high price too. Leon accused us of undertaking the attack on Constantinople at the behest of the Pope in Rome -- of being his agents. As a punishment, he ordered that henceforth the Church of Hellas be administered from Constantinople, rather than Rome.

"When Leon died, his iconoclast policies were continued by his son Constantine, and on his death by his son Leon. With much of the opposition to iconoclasm being centered in the monasteries, the latter Leon ordered them closed and the monastic habit forbidden. Instead of holy icons depicting the life of saints, paintings of flowers, fruit and birds were ordered to decorate the churches of the empire.

"What madness!

"Empress Irene, of blessed memory, finally put an end to the travesty. On the death of her husband, she convened a council of bishops that ruled iconoclasm a heresy, ordered the restoration of the monasteries and urgedthe faithful to resume the practice of venerating icons.

"My brothers and sisters in Christ!" continued Gregorios.

"We are not done with iconoclasm. No, not yet! Once again the heresy has raised its ugly head. We are in the midst of another cycle of persecution by religious fanatics, pursuing rules of their own. Our holy images are again being destroyed and their defenders fiercely punished. Bishops, clergy, and monks who refuse to comply with the decrees of the iconoclast emperor are being deposed, banished, and even tortured. The icon of Christ hanging in front of the Imperial palace, which had been restored by Empress Irene, has again been removed. A new generation of sinners is occupying the throne. You know their names: Leon, Michael, and our present emperor, the worthless Theophilus.

"When will it all end? Pray my brothers and sisters, pray for our Empress Theodora, for she is our only hope. Pray that she will follow in the footsteps of Empress Irene before, revoke the iconoclast laws, and finally bring our people the spiritual peace which they so richly deserve."

"Was it Theodora, Karyatis, who finally restored the icons?"

"Yes. On the death of her husband, she revoked all decrees outlawing icons and other religious symbols. And on a Sunday, that I believe Christians refer to as the First Sunday of Lent, she brought them back to the Church of Haghia Sophia in Constantinople, in a solemn procession. An Athenian who happened to be present for the event described it as awe-inspiring, with hundreds of clergy, many in tears, entering the famed Cathedral with their beloved icons held high above their heads."

"I would have loved to been there, Karyatis."

"It must have been majestic! The Byzantines, Sophia, were great at organizing religious processions. During my days on the Acropolis, I witnessed a very large number of them, whether to honor a saint or pay homage to an emperor. My neighbor the Church of Panaghia Athiniotissa was especially tireless in this regard, which allowed me a front view of the proceedings. I was there, for instance, when Emperors Konstas and later Vassilios the Voulgaroktonos came to Athens. Their processions through the agora, then up the hill to the Acropolis, were enormously triumphant affairs. Truly grand!"

The visit by Emperor Konstas to Athens came as a real surprise. The emperor had been engaged in a long struggle with the Lombards, when he suddenly decided to bring the war to the enemy's home turf by invading Sicily. Departing Constantinople at the head of a naval expedition, he first cruised down the Aegean, then around the island of Evia before landing in Piraeus. He must have liked living in Athens, because he spent the following six months there. To the city, long since forgotten as a center of the arts and learning, the presence of a Byzantine emperor in their midst was an enormously important event.

It did not take long for Emperor Konstas, his court and bodyguards, to decide where in Athens precisely they wanted to be. The Acropolis, converted earlier into a fortress by Emperor Justinian, offered great safety and its sights were unsurpassed. The emperor had barely concluded his prayers on the day of his arrival at the Church of Panaghia Athiniotissa, when he announced to the crowd present that henceforth the local bishop's official residence near the church would be that of the emperor. Konstas loved catching the sights of the city, and would visit regularly temples or other buildings from the classical period that still remained intact. The Byzantine emperor, however, was no different than earlier visitors to the city when it came to Hellenic art. Whenever he would notice something that he liked particularly well, he would order it confiscated and shipped to his palace back home.

After departing Hellas, Konstas confronted the Lombards in Sicily, and then traveled to Syracuse and Rome. Returning to Constantinople, he met a tragic death in the hands of an assassin, as did so many other Byzantine emperors before and after him. Rumors were that his killer was one of his servants, who drove a knife into his heart while assisting him to take a bath.

The visit by Emperor Vassilios Voulgaroktonos (i.e. the Bulgars'slayer) took place many years later. As in the case of the Konstas visit, it was an especially important event to the sleepy town that was then Athens. Vassilios had a single purpose for coming. He wanted to thank the *Theotokos* for helping him defeat the Bulgarians, and forcing them to abandon Hellas once and forever, a goal that had eluded him for over thirty years. In preparation for his visit, a dome and three small chapels were added to the Church of Panaghia Athiniotissa, and numerous important guests, generals, bishops, judges, and others were invited from all corners of the empire. The emperor's arrival was especially triumphant, with enormous crowds cheering and otherwise acclaiming the Voulgaroktonos emperor. Inside the Church, Vassilios prostrated himself before the icon of the *Theotokos,* kissing it in the custom of his faith, and then presented it with numerous gifts of precious stones captured during his Bulgarian campaigns. Included was a large golden dove, signifying the Holy Spirit.

Personally, Sophia, I got carried away at first and liked Vassilios, despite his unsightly looks and arrogant personality. But after hearing of the horrible crime that he had committed at the end of the Bulgarian campaign, I didn't ever want to hear his name mentioned again.

In case you are not familiar with the event, it appears that at his last battle, the emperor had taken 15,000 Bulgarian soldiers as prisoners. Vassilios was so filled with hatred toward his old enemy, he ordered all 15,000 to be blinded -- blinded, Sophia. Only one soldier in every one hundred was allowed to retain one good eye, to lead the remaining prisoners back home to Bulgaria. According to stories circulating in Constantinople at the time, and which eventually reached Athens, the Bulgarian king suffered a grand seizure at the sight of his blind soldiers, and died.

"What a horrible deed, Karyatis. But I am not surprised. Even today, humans act at times with beastly brutality toward other humans."

The Byzantine years were especially grim, Sophia, as Hellas was invaded repeatedly from the north. Not all invaders were cruel of course, but some were. Athenians referred to all invaders as barbarians, because they dressed differently, spoke strange languages, and worshipped arcane gods.

Watching it all from my position, it appeared as if the Byzantines were forever involved in a state of war. They were either trying to acquire new lands, or were defending the frontiers of the empire against invaders. I would hear accounts of these conflicts from refugees who would crowd into the city, and the safety of its walls, whenever invaders from the north crossed the narrow pass at Thermopylae, or otherwise reached our neighboring city of Thebes.

The conduct of the invaders varied widely. The early Slavs, for instance, were people in search of land on which to live and raise their families. They kept clear of large cities, and hardly ever showed an inclination to establish a kingdom of their own. Other invaders, however, such as the later Slavs, the Avars, and Bulgarians entered Thessaly and Attica in anger. Their looting and killing of innocents was reminiscent of the crimes committed by the Goths and Visigoths in earlier years. At times, Byzantium fought long and hard campaigns to either push the invaders back, or to allow them to remain in place on condition of suspending all fighting and paying an annual tribute to the Byzantine treasury.

The people that the Byzantines found the hardest to subjugate were the Bulgarians. Despite their conversion to Christianity by the two brother monks, Methodios and Cyrilos, and numerous other Byzantine actions designed to gain their favor, the Bulgarians persisted in invading Hellas, once even reaching as far south as the city of Corinth. Leading the 30-year struggle to finally subdue the Bulgarians was Vassilios the Voulgaroktonos. He attacked them without mercy, and as we saw earlier punished them brutally at the end.

Athens was spared major destruction from these invasions. In many ways it fared better than the Imperial capital of Constantinople, which also was repeatedly attacked (but never entered) by invading armies from the north, east and south.

Persians, Avars, Bulgarians, and even Arabs, were successful at one time or another of besieging Constantinople, only to be decisively turned back by the "fire," the superb Byzantine defensive weapon that had the property of burning on water.

"It is truly amazing, Karyatis, how much you can recollect!"

"Thank you. If you have time, there are two additional very significant events of that era that I would like to discuss with you, Sophia. They are both religious in nature and account for much of the resentment that people in the East harbored toward Rome."

"The schism of the Churches?"

"Yes, and also the Crusades.

"I'll try to be impartial in describing these events to you, although frankly during my years on the Acropolis I heard mostly the Eastern Orthodox point of view. After the Church of the Panaghia Athiniotissa, however, was converted into a Latin Church, I did have the opportunity to hear also Rome's account."

"As an Anglican, Karyatis, I have no strong views on these matters one way or another."

The Orthodox-Latin dispute had been brewing for a very long time, Sophia, so it was only natural that I would hear bits and pieces on events as they occurred. The early disputes were relatively minor, the result of different customs and traditions practiced by the two sides, and the fact that East and West had grown steadily apart since the breakup of the Roman Empire. With the passage of time, however, more fundamental issues surfaced which the two sides were either unwilling, or unable to reconcile. Headstrong actions by Rome and Constantinople, compounded by scathing rhetoric, gave rise to much anger and resentment at both ends of the Christian church. The anger -- hostility is probably a better term -- reached its peak during the Fourth Crusades, when the crusaders considered by many in the East as being "the soldiers of the Pope," captured and ransacked the Byzantine capital of Constantinople, and its co-capital Thessaloniki. By all accounts, the plunder and destruction that followed were unparalleled in the history of both cities.

In the aftermath of the tragedy, all voices in Athens that formerly counseled unity and reconciliation with the West suddenly were silenced. The only voices left were those of angry men, both lay and clergy, who used every opportunity to chastise and rebuke Rome and its leadership. One such irate voice was that of Archmandrite Ieronymos, of the Church of Panaghia Athiniotissa. Father Ieronymos was a Hellene from Asia Minor, who had studied theology in Constantinople during the reign of the Komninos dynasty. An expert on issues of dogma, he had been assigned duty early on in his career as the secretary of the Ecumenical Patriarch. But he was soon eased out of that position, and exiled to Athens, when his extreme views on Rome became known.

"The root of our problems with the West," I recall him telling his assembled flock angrily one evening, "is Rome's insistence of having the final say on all matters of church policy; all matters mind you, from dogma to administration, to the selection of our Patriarch. Where is it written, I ask you, that Rome should have this authority and that the Pope could interfere in the internal affairs of the other patriarchates?

"Years ago, when the Holy Synod in Constantinople elected Photios to serve as our Patriarch, a man of great virtue, wisdom, and ability, Pope Nicholas rejected his election charging that it had been irregular. Why? The election of Patriarch Photios was irregular, but the crowning by the Pope of that barbarian, Charlemagne, as Emperor of the West was regular?

"There is more!

"Without ever consulting anyone in the East, the Pope introduced changes in the church dogma, and took actions that are canonically improper. He inserted the word "filioque" in the eighth article of the Creed (that is the one dealing with the Holy Spirit), thus redefining the Holy Spirit as proceeding from the Father as well as the Son. He has come up with the concept of the Purgatory, distinct from Hell, and has insisted on beginning the Great Lent each year on a Wednesday, rather than Monday as is proper.

"Now my friends, we have tried repeatedly to negotiate with Rome the issues that divide us, only to be rebuffed by them, again and again. We complained when Rome tried to detach the Church of Bulgaria from the jurisdiction of the Patriarchate, and complained again when the Pope interfered in areas outside his jurisdiction. What did we receive in return? A formal excommunication!

"This sacrilegious act occurred on the grounds of the Holy Church of Haghia Sophia, in Constantinople. Cardinal Humbert had been visiting the Imperial capital at the invitation of the emperor for the purpose of restoring friendly relations between the two churches. But the Cardinal not once asked to meet the emperor or the Patriarch. Instead, one bright morning he left an edict of excommunication on the Altar of the Church of Haghia Sophia, and departed hastily. What other course did our Patriarch have but to respond in turn with his own anathema?"

Listen now, Sophia, to the voice of Rome, as presented by Monsignor Theodore, the Roman Catholic priest who succeeded Ieronymos at the Church of Panaghia Athiniotissa, after it was converted to a Latin Church.

"Athenians! The facts are not as the fanatics in the East would have you believe. When Pope Nicholas refused to concur in the selection of Photios, as Patriarch of Constantinople, he was merely following established church practice of having each new Patriarch seek the concurrence of his fellow Patriarchs before assuming his throne. Photios was a layman with no prior religious experience, so it was only natural for the Holy Father to take the position that he did. How could such a man suddenly be elevated to the highest rank of the church? I'll tell you how! The emperor was behind the move. And, how did Photios respond to the Pope's displeasure? He ordered him deposed.

"It is ironic, but Patriarch Photios was removed from his post by the same emperor who had him appointed. Thereupon, a Holy Synod, held in Constantinople, acknowledged the Pope's supremacy over all other Patriarchs, even on decisions sanctioned by an Ecumenical Council. Why then is Constantinople complaining of the Holy Father's involvement on matters of faith in the East? Without his counsel, without his steady leadership, senseless heresies and discords are likely to surface again.

"Do you recall Byzantium during the era of iconoclasm? Do you remember the churches defiled, the priests and bishops thrown into jail, and monasteries destroyed? Rome tried repeatedly to persuade that misguided Emperor Leon, that the practice of having religious images in our churches was in line with Christian dogma. But to no avail.

"As for Cardinal Humbert's visit to Constantinople, it occurred in the aftermath of the closing of numerous Latin churches in the Imperial capital. On orders of the Holy Father, the Cardinal attempted to resolve this and the other issues separating the two churches with the Orthodox authorities. He met nothing but intransigence, especially on the doctrine of the Holy Spirit. He deposited thereupon the edict condemning the Patriarch, and his Church, and returned to Rome. These are the facts, my friends. This is precisely what happened!

"Now in the years since, we have tried repeatedly to reach out to the authorities in Constantinople, only to discover to our sorrow that reconciliation is impossible. The Church authorities appear agreeable to a settlement, but the rank and file Christians in the East are not. They no longer consider us as their brothers in Christ."

"Despite the lapse of time, Karyatis, this schism between East and West continues. The mutual anathemas have been withdrawn, but little additional progress has been made toward unity. Then, there is also that episode in history known as the Fourth Crusade which the people in the East are having great difficulty forgetting."

My knowledge of the Fourth Crusade, Sophia, comes primarily from Chrysseline, an Athenian woman, a governess, who had been living in the home of a wealthy Byzantine family in the Imperial capital when the tragic events unfolded. Abused by crusaders, beaten and raped, she managed finally to escape the hell that Constantinople had become, and returned to Athens along with a dozen other Hellenes. Deprived of family and friends, Chryssaline walked the streets of the city for weeks aimlessly, before finding refuge inside my temple. She was good company and until her passing many years later, remained my neighbor, best friend, and companion.

"It is such a great irony, Karyatis," I recall her lamenting many years later, "that glorious Constantinople, the Imperial capital and seat of Orthodoxy, was laid waste not by some alien and barbarian people from Asia, but by fellow Christians from Venice and France. By soldiers in the service of the Pope! By Christians, whose avowed purpose for taking up arms had been to free the Holy Land from the infidels. A noble goal, but one for which at the end they had nothing to show for but shame and dishonor.

"As for myself, I'll curse these men in all eternity. May their heinous crimes never be forgotten. Not only did they slaughter, rape, and maim thousands of their fellow Christians, but they also destroyed the jewel that was Constantinople - a city more beautiful, more sparkling, than even Athens was during the age of Pericles.

"They plundered moreover the greatest collection of Hellenic and Christian art ever assembled in one place. I am not exaggerating! No other city in the entire world could match the Imperial capital's wealth, beauty and power. First-time visitors would stare incredulously at its huge palaces, vast cathedrals with their gilded domes, its glorious monuments, and forests of sculpture. Do you recall the immense statue of Athena Promachos that once stood here at the entrance to the Acropolis, the work of Phidias? That, too, graced Constantinople in a magnificent open area not far from Haghia Sophia, along with hundreds of other marble and bronze statues of Hellenic origin.

"As for the Haghia Sophia itself, what can I say Karyatis? Before it was depleted by the hordes, who referred to themselves as Crusaders, it contained some of the holiest relics of Christian piety, and was adorned by enormous amounts of gold, silver, jewels and other precious stones. Its icons and mosaics were unequalled in their beauty and elegance.

"Today Byzantium is a city in captivity, devoid of its former glory, beauty, wealth and art. In a demented irrational display of barbarism, the vandals from the West smashed, shattered, wrecked every statue, and every monument they came across. Complete insanity, I am telling you.

"The Fourth Crusade, Karyatis, began with the best of intentions. France was to provide the manpower, and Venice the ships for transporting the men and weapons required to liberate the Holy Land. But as preparations were being finalized a Byzantine prince by the name of Alexis, appeared on the scene. His father, Emperor Isaac, he reported, had been dethroned and blinded and was being kept in the dungeons in Constantinople. Would the crusaders be willing to assist him in reclaiming the throne, by escorting him back to the gates of the city? The people in the capital were opposed to the new rulers and would support his return with great enthusiasm. In return for the favor, Alexis was prepared to provide the crusaders with the required money, provisions, and manpower for the conquest of the Holy Land.

"The Doge of Venice, technically in charge of the venture, could not refuse such a generous offer, and soon the crusader fleet appeared before the walls of Constantinople. But the promised popular support for Prince Alexis never materialized; he was very young, a naïve youth, full of ambition but no ability. The people ignored him. Eventually, after the crusaders feinted an armed assault on the city, the usurper emperor fled and Alexis ascended the throne. With the fleeing emperor, however, fled also the entire Byzantine treasury.

"Strapped for funds, Alexis was unable to make good on his promises. He did succeed, however, in raising enough money to provide the crusaders with food and shelter, during the winter months that followed. As for the crusaders themselves, they settled in for the duration being reluctant to either leave the city without the men, supplies, and gold which had been promised them or to return home to Venice.

"Before long, anger at the crusaders began building up in the city. People wondered how much longer Constantinople was expected to feed a foreign army. There were reports of riots and plots to remove Alexis.

"When he was finally removed from office, and killed along with his father Isaac, Alexios Dukas, a nobleman known for his anti-Western views assumed the throne. His first order of business was to order the strengthening of the Byzantine army, a clear signal to the crusaders that they had overextended their stay. Soon, war between the two sides seemed unavoidable.

"It took but a few days for the crusaders to overcome the Byzantine defenses. What followed was one of the most shocking devastations of a city in the annals of warfare. The victorious crusaders murdered, pillaged and destroyed everything in their path, snatching up whatever of value they could find and demolishing what they could not carry. It was horrible, Karyatis. Nothing escaped their anger - churches, monasteries, homes, public buildings, all fell victim to their rage.

"My master who was a wealthy importer of grain from Odessa, his wife, and two sons became early victims of the rampage, when they attempted to stop a group of crusaders from entering their house. I witnessed their murders while hidden in a tool shed in the horses' stable. After searching their bodies for money, or other valuables, removing their personal belongings and looting the house, the mob departed.

"I don't know to this day, Karyatis, how I succeeded in finding passage on a small boat for the trip back home. All I can recall is a sobbing elderly man sitting next to me, retelling us in a state of total shock the sacking of Haghia Sophia. Apparently, he had taken refuge in the Great Church only to witness crusaders on horseback in the soleas removing sacred vessels, jewels, chandeliers and other works of art. It was true mayhem, he kept repeating."

"That, pretty much tells the story of Athens during the Byzantine era, Sophia. There is much more, of course, but with Edward being back in town we'd better move on."

"It shouldn't affect our schedule, Karyatis. For a while at least, Edward will not be having much free time for me. He'll be busy trying to catch up with his teaching and research activities."

"You will be then here tomorrow?"

"Yes, bright and early. What will you have for me then?"

"The story of the Frankish years. Three boring centuries of French, Catalan, and Florentine rule of Athens, when nothing much happened. The Ottomans came afterwards."

"It was during the Ottoman period that you were removed from your temple, and forcibly transferred here, correct?

"Yes."

"When we reach that part of your story, Karyatis, I may be able to help with details you might not be familiar with. Since getting to know you, I have been reading on the life and times of the man who was responsible."

"You mean, Elgin?"

"Yes, and also on others who were involved in that infamous art heist," Sophia answered with a smile.

"Sophia! I cannot believe that you've said that. You do agree, that forcing me here was a case of outright theft?"

"Yes. But why are you surprised, Karyatis? You have been a good teacher and I a compliant pupil," she answered, a sparkle of mischief in her eyes, as she was leaving.

VIII

LORD ELGIN AND HIS MANSION

True to her word, Sophia is among the first visitors today. But instead of taking up her position behind her canvas, as she always does, I see her heading toward the guard station in the next gallery. Three men are manning the station this morning, and Sophia stops to chat with them briefly.

How unusual. Normally, only one guard is on duty in Room 20. Is the museum expecting another important visitor today?

Although distance makes it difficult for me to hear what is being said, I can tell that the talk between the guards is extremely animated. One of the men keeps pointing at the room where the Parthenon sculptures are exhibited. Another, is trying to reach someone on his cellular phone.

I note how radiant Sophia again looks this morning. The smart brown suit she is wearing, not only accentuates her graceful posture, it makes her look absolutely fabulous. I wonder why she is dressed so formally. Could she be having a social engagement later today?

She is finally walking over in my direction. I can hardly wait.

"What's happening Sophia," I inquire. "Why all the excitement this morning? Is an important visitor expected?"

"The wife of the Vice-President of the United States is due some time after lunch, Karyatis. But this is not what the commotion is all about.

"It appears, that early this morning about fifty Greek students from local universities showed up at the front gate of the Museum on Great Russell Street. They are carrying signs, and chanting slogans that must be dear to your heart -- asking that the Parthenon sculptures be returned to Greece. The security contingent at the front gate was slow to react, and about a dozen students have managed to chain themselves to the museum's front gate. TV crews have arrived and the event is being beamed across the world on CNN. In the meantime, the police are working feverishly to free the students."

"I am confused, Sophia. What is Greece? Why are these students, whom you call Greek, campaigning for the return of the Parthenon sculptures to Athens?"

"You don't know, Karyatis? Greece is the name now being used for Hellas. The nation that you knew as Hellas is now known as Greece."

"Why? I prefer the old name so much better."

"As I was saying, the police are hoping to free the students and escort them out of the area before the American visitor arrives. She will probably be travelling with a large entourage of aides and media people. Having students demonstrating at the front gate of the museum does not add to its image."

"Did you get a chance to see the students, when you came in this morning?"

"Only from a distance. I, along with all other visitors, was directed to enter through the entrance on Montague Place. From a distance, the students appeared agitated and so were the police who were trying desperately to contain them, and to establish some sense of order."

"You will tell me, Sophia, if anything develops later?"

"You know that I will, Karyatis. Besides, things should be returning to normal soon."

Somehow Sophia's last comment does not ring true. If order is being restored, why the increased vigilance? Why the extra guards?

Any minute now she'll want me to resume with my story, but my heart is not in it. Apprehension has overtaken me over the events outside. How are the students doing, I wonder? Are the police being hard on them? Has their protest had the hoped-for impact? Uncanny as it might seem, will the authorities heed the students' plea, and agree to returning the Parthenon sculptures back to Hellas? I mean, Greece?

And, what about me?

Through the large doors that allow visitors entry to my gallery, I note a young couple. They are clinging on each other as if in an embrace, still their expression is sad. Hardly, the typical museum visitors.

"There was absolutely no need for that kind of police violence, Roger," I hear the young woman whisper into her companion's ear. "Attacking the students with clubs! Why, for God's sake? I actually saw a policeman pounding a young man with his club, after he had fallen to the ground.

"You saw it yourself, Roger," she continued. "These students never threatened anyone! They had a message to deliver, which they hoped the world would hear and take notice. They meant no harm, didn't damage Museum property, or abuse any of its visitors. They were a lot more respectful and courteous than visitors occasionally are."

I cannot believe what I am hearing. The police are using clubs against the students? How cruel! That would explain why the visiting couple looks so downcast.

"The students probably violated some city ordinance, Sarah, that prohibits demonstrations on Museum grounds," I hear Roger explain. "Besides, the students' message -- returning the Parthenon sculptures to Greece -- is anathema to the authorities of the British Museum."

"The demonstration must still be going on, Roger," I heard her remark, as they passed before me on the way to the next chamber. "I think, I am hearing what sounds like police sirens."

"I will be leaving early today, Karyatis," Sophia suddenly announces, "but should be back tomorrow. I have an appointment with the editor of an art magazine, who is doing a story on my current show at a local gallery. He wants to interview me, and has also asked that I provide him with digital prints of my work for inclusion in his article. We'll probably work through dinner because the magazine has a very tight deadline."

"Must be exciting, seeing a story about your work in print."

"It is a confidence builder."

"How about Edward? Is he still trying to catch up with his backlog?"

"Yes. We are having an anniversary later this week, and he's promised, no matter what, an entire afternoon and evening together. Apparently, his sabbatical in Washington really set him back in his work."

"He sounds like a very busy man."

"That he is. Between his position as Administrator of the university's Department of History, and Director of its Institute of Historical Research, Edward hardly has a free moment to himself. It is his nature, also to want to become involved in all kinds of historical activities, such as his recent study of Byzantine coins. What can I say? He lives only for history."

"For you, too, Sophia, I am sure. Don't be modest."

"You are right, I guess.

"Edward is so darn dedicated and also such a fantastic teacher, he is forever in demand by students, history scholars, and other members of the faculty. And he does not consider his day complete unless he has spent some time working on a one-to-one basis with some of his students, monitoring their development, and in general acting as their personal tutor. The Institute of Historical Research is situated in the heart of Bloomsbury, close to the University and the British Library. It is of course a world-renowned center for historical research", she added, beaming with pride.

"But, enough about Edward, Karyatis, I think we should return to your story. With the American visitor due any moment now, and my engagement with the magazine publisher later this evening, we'll be short on time today."

"I can start, of course.

"But Sophia, I've been wondering. Why not take a break from my story? Frankly, I'd love to hear from you regarding some of the things that you've been able to discover in your readings. About Elgin, I mean. The thought has always haunted me: what possessed the man to want to strip the Parthenon clean of all that beautiful art, and to also include me in his loot?"

"I'll be glad to fill in the blanks for you, Karyatis, but please keep in mind, that I might not be able to answer all your questions. There's still a lot more reading that I must do."

To start out with – and please don't take me wrong, Karyatis -- based on what I've read thus far, Lord Elgin wasn't really an evil person. Overly ambitious and vain, yes; an opportunist, yes; allowing himself to be influenced by others, sure; but evil, he was not.

And let me also disengage you from the prevailing notion, that Elgin somehow had planned from the very outset to exploit his position as His Majesty's Ambassador to the Ottoman court to raid the Parthenon, for the benefit of his home in Scotland. The facts are quite different.

Lord Elgin bears, of course, major responsibility for the theft. But so do also his close aide and confidant, the Reverend Philip Hunt, who was instrumental in swaying him on the need for "rescuing" the treasures of the Parthenon, and also the Turkish officials, who stood by idly while the Elgin team was ransacking the Acropolis on the basis of a very ambiguous directive or firman from Constantinople.

I don't want to get ahead of myself.

As a young man Lord Elgin, born Thomas Bruce to a prominent Scottish family, made all the right career moves of a British nobleman. He received a fine education at home and in Paris, served in the military including service as commander of his own regiment, got himself elected as Representative Peer of Scotland, and also married a wealthy woman, the beautiful Mary Nisbet. Early on, he also joined the diplomatic service, receiving extraordinary assignments in Vienna, Brussels, and Berlin, culminating with his appointment to the much-sought after post of Ambassador to Constantinople. Elgin, then only thirty-two, was clearly on his way up.

Elgin's marriage to Mary Nisbet took place a year before his appointment to Constantinople. It was motivated, undoubtedly, by her beauty, but also the fact that Mary was heiress to a very large fortune. Not wanting to be outdone by her wealth and despite his own tight financial condition, Lord Elgin promised his bride a handsome new mansion back home in Scotland. To plan the details of his mansion he selected Thomas Harrison, a neo-classical architect.

Harrison, who had studied in Rome suggested to Elgin that a neo-classical mansion would be most appropriate for the occasion. But, before being able to prepare the necessary drawings, it would be helpful he said, if he had detailed drawings and three-dimensional plaster casts of ancient Greek architecture and sculptures. As Ambassador to Constantinople whose jurisdiction included also the territory of Hellas, Harrison suggested, Elgin would be in a unique position to obtain the required information, and in the process also introduce the people of Britain to the classical art of Hellas.

Elgin, a man of little artistic appreciation but always quick to agree with any scheme that would advance his social or political standing, went along willingly. His term of office in Constantinople, he resolved, would be dedicated to the service of the arts. The idea so enthused him, that when public funds for the project were denied him he decided to carry out the work using his own resources.

Remember Karyatis, there is no evidence to this point, that Elgin was thinking of anything more than preparing drawings and plaster casts of Greek art, for use by his architect in the design of his home in Scotland; by extension also, for the British public to enjoy. The decision to physically remove the art was made later.

His appointments before departing for his new post offer ample evidence of this. After selecting William Richard Hamilton to serve as his personal secretary, and the Reverend Philip Hunt as his chaplain, Elgin set out to find painters and molders qualified to do the work. Had he intended to remove sculptures and ship them home, he would have recruited stone cutters instead. Unable to meet the financial demands of qualified artists in Britain he turned his sights next to Italy.

In Italy, Elgin hired a landscape painter by the name of Giovanni Battista Lusieri, to whom he assigned the overall responsibility for the operations on the Acropolis. To him, and his personal secretary Hamilton, Elgin also entrusted the recruitment of the remaining artists required for the project.

The first appointment by Lusieri and Hamilton went to a strange sort of a fellow, a painter named Feodor Ivanovitch. Two architectural draftsmen, Vincenzo Balestra and Sebastian Ittar, were hired next, and also Bernadino Ledus and Vincenzo Rosati, who were molders by profession. Their job, as was explained to them, was to carefully measure every ancient monument on the Acropolis and to make plaster casts of the more interesting ones.

While Lord Elgin, his wife and the Reverend Hunt headed for Constantinople, the team entrusted to prepare the drawings and casts of Greek art arrived in Athens. Needless to say, the Hellas that they found was a forlorn and spiritless country, the city of Athens even smaller and dirtier than earlier visitors had reported it to be, and the Acropolis suffering from the aftereffect of neglect and abuse in the hands of foreign invaders.

As you yourself can recall Karyatis, all temples on the Acropolis had seen changes during the years of Turkish rule. The Parthenon had been converted into a mosque, your own temple the Erechteum served as both a harem and an ammunition depot, and the Propylaea were used as a base for the emplacement of a cannon battery. A "Disdar," or military governor was now in charge of the Acropolis and its military facilities, while a "Voivode," or governor was responsible for the civil administration of the city.

From the very outset Elgin's team encountered major difficulties in its dealings with the Disdar, who demanded the payment of five guineas per day, for each worker, with the stipulation that all work had to be performed at ground level. Drawings of temples could be made, but not castings, and neither could scaffolding be erected which was essential for examining the upper sections of the temples. Presumably, scaffolds would have allowed the foreign workers to look inside the many surrounding Turkish homes, and the women residing in them. Before long the Disdar announced that the team could no longer continue its work on the Acropolis without the appropriate permission, or "firman" from Constantinople.

Much of the controversy over the removal of the Parthenon sculptures revolves over the firman, which Lord Elgin was able to secure from the Turkish authorities in his capacity as His Majesty's Ambassador. The language of the firman, and its timing, raise a host of language and legal issues, all having a bearing on the controversy.

"My watch tells me, Karyatis, that I should be leaving soon; I don't want to be late for my appointment with the magazine editor. We can return to Elgin, if you wish at our next session. But remember, you are not finished as yet with your story. You still haven't told me of "those boring Frankish and Ottoman years when nothing much happened." I believe that's what you had called them, right?"

"Yes. But do you have time, Sophia, for a brief question?"

"A brief one."

"How important in Elgin's decision to remove the Parthenon sculptures was his desire to decorate his mansion in Scotland?"

"Once Elgin had been persuaded by the Reverend Hunt that the art on the Acropolis had to be "rescued" from further damage, and that the permit granted to him by the Turkish authorities could be interpreted as allowing him to do that, he made the beautification of his home in Scotland his first priority. His earlier goal of preparing drawings and castings to be used by his architect, and for the viewing pleasure of the British public, was all but abandoned."

"Please don't mind me interrupting you again, Sophia; but

I do need to understand why I am here.

"It all started, you say, with Harrison the architect asking Elgin to provide him with sketches of Hellenic art, and of three dimensional casts of sculptures for use in the design of his mansion? Harrison did not ask that individual statues be removed, right?"

"He never did. In fact, when later Harrison heard that sculptures were indeed being removed from the temples of the Acropolis, he broke off all contacts with Elgin."

"So, I am here because Dr. Hunt somehow convinced Elgin that the Parthenon art had to be "rescued" from the hands of those who did not appreciate it?"

"Yes, and also from the ravages of time."

"Did Harrison, ever request specifically that a sketch be made of my temple, my sisters, or of me?"

"Not to my knowledge. Much later, however, after Elgin had resolved to remove all the art that he could from the Acropolis, he did entertain the idea of removing also the entire Karyatis portico from your temple, ...the entire portico mind you, not just you. The obvious difficulty with this undertaking was locating a British man of war capable of transporting the precious load to London. Elgin even wrote to the Commander of the British forces in the Mediterranean pleading the case of moving to Britain "these beautiful models of ancient art." But he was turned down, to his bitter disappointment."

"So, I am here because of that rascal Reverend Hunt? I think I remember him, Sophia. Almost every morning when he was in Athens he would take a stroll on the Acropolis, usually unaccompanied, that would bring him by my temple.

He was short, stocky and was dressed in a clergyman's garb. He appeared very interested in art, always carrying a note-book with him on which he recorded his impressions. Little did I know!"

"Don't blame him alone, Kayatis. It was Elgin, after all, who was in charge of the entire operation. He could have rejected Hunt's pleas, if he wanted to, and you'd still be on the Acropolis where you long to be."

IX

FRANKS AND OTTOMANS

When we left our story, Sophia, a couple of days ago the crusaders had conquered Constantinople, were raiding the city of its treasures, killing and abusing its citizens, and humiliating with unprecedented brutality the few Orthodox clergy who had remained behind.

In the weeks that followed the news from the former Byzantine capital got even worse. Rumors began circulating that the crusaders had abandoned their original plan of freeing the Holy Land from the dominion of non-Christians, choosing instead to stay and enjoy life in Constantinople. Proof came soon enough, when they proceeded to partition into three separate political entities, the parts of the empire that they had conquered. First, they established a new kingdom -- the Kingdom of Constantinople, based on the capital city and including Thrace, and several former Byzantine lands in Asia Minor. Next, they rewarded Venice for its participation in the Crusade by granting it ports on mainland Hellas, on several large Aegean islands, and on Crete. As a mercantile powerhouse, Venice's only interest was for territory having a trading potential. The remaining Byzantine lands, including the city of Athens were organized into the Kingdom of Thessaloniki, under the control of Marquis Boniface.

The new political map of Hellas did not last long. Soon it was redrawn again, when political pressures forced the Marquis Boniface to transfer the control of the city of Athens and its surrounding area of Attica to Otto de la Roche, a friend and fellow knight from Burgundy.

Thus began the Frankish period of Athens, during which the city was ruled initially by the Franks, and later by Catalans, and Florentines. The period lasted well over two hundred years, at which time Hellas and all that remained of the Latin and Byzantine lands fell into the hands of the Ottomans. By far the most ruthless of all Latin occupiers were the Catalans. Traders by profession, they were also ferocious mercenaries who would sell their services to the highest bidder. The Catalans instituted a tyrannical regime in Athens, including a very oppressive legal system, and the mandatory use of the Spanish language in all commercial transactions.

By contrast, the Florentines were most generous toward the city and its inhabitants. Their rulers, members of the Acciajuolo family, were wealthy bankers with a keen appreciation of Athenian history and culture. They learned the language spoken by the people, married Athenian maidens, and displayed their affection for the city in a number of ways.

I have few recollections of the Frankish years, Sophia. The one that I can never erase from memory, however, was the decision by Otto de la Roche to erect a medieval fortress at the entrance of the Acropolis, near the Propylaea. That monstrosity changed not only the physical appearance of the area, but also its very essence: from a sanctuary where gods could be venerated in a serene and dignified setting , to a fortified stronghold designed for war.

Can you imagine knights on horseback near the Parthenon, or horses being fed and groomed in front of my temple? It was precisely what happened. Once the fortress, horse stables, and associated storage bunkers, had been completed, the "Sir" of Athens, and his court, took up residence on the Acropolis. The move involving several hundred men, their weapons and families, was followed by the traditional symbols of medieval life -- the training of knights, jousting exhibitions, tournaments, feasts, etc. Incidentally, "Sir" of Athens was the title given initially to Otto de la Roche; later he was elevated to the rank of a "Duke."

From what I could gather in discussions by Athenians visiting my temple, mostly everyone in the city resented bitterly the indignity of a fortress on the Acropolis. Otherwise, Athenians tolerated the Latin rule fairly well, despite the fact that most foreign rulers did not speak their language, or understood their culture and mores. Taxes paid to the new rulers were not much heavier than those levied earlier by the Byzantines, and Athenian men were seldom inducted into the military service of the dukedom. During the Catalan years, common sense dictated that everyone be humble and submissive to the authorities. At other times, however, Athenians went about their lives with little regard for the foreigners in their midst, ignoring the goings-on in the castle where the center of power was, and the near continuous infighting between competing knights. As during the Byzantine era, their city was small and insignificant and second in ranking to Thebes, its neighbor, that served as the political capital of the region.

My first exposure to medieval practices and customs, Sophia, was confusing to say the least. There were so many different men milling around the area, many with strange titles and wearing odd-looking insignia and uniforms. It was outright impossible for me to tell them apart. My predicament was resolved when not far from my location, an elderly French knight from Lyon, begun instructing his grandson Henri on the intricacies of knighthood and the medieval way of life. Without the information that I was able to glean from him, the Frankish period would still have been a deep mystery to me.

"A knight, Henri," the old man informed his young ward, at the start of the daily training session, "must always display superior skill and bravery in battle. You cannot receive your sword and be formally vested with the rank of a knight, until you provide proof that you possess these qualities. As one of noble birth -- you are after all, a close relative of Prince Henri, the ruler of the Kingdom of Constantinople -- becoming a knight is not a choice that you have. It is your responsibility, before family and God.

"As a fourteen-year old boy and a mere page all this may sound overwhelming to you. But Duke William, to whom we all owe allegiance, has been greatly impressed with your progress. You have learned to be courteous and obedient to the elders in the castle, and are showing promise of growing into a proud and commanding nobleman. The duke has therefore directed that you advance to the next stage, that of being a squire. As a squire, Henri, you will be instructed on how to act as a knight and grow into full manhood.

"We will begin by examining the armor that you will be wearing. And since, much of your time as a knight will be spent on horseback, we will pay particular attention to the various shields and trappings needed to keep your horse safe and unhurt in battle. As you progress, you will also be taught the use of the bow and arrow for hunting"…

"I already know how, papa," interrupted the boy, anxious to show off some of his acquired skills to his elder relative.

"I am glad, Henri. Later on, of course, you'll have to become intimately familiar with your principal weapons as a knight -- the sword, the axe, and the mace - and how they could help you overcome your enemies. You must master the use of these weapons especially while on horseback, using one arm to control your horse, while keeping the other free for your weapons. As you progress you will also be introduced to the art of jousting, an athletic contest, which must come as second nature to any well trained knight.

"On the very day that you will be knighted, trumpets will blare to announce the arrival of your opponent, and you will have your first opportunity to prove to your peers your skill in jousting. The field will be crowded and people will have come from throughout the dukedom to observe the event. You'll have to be at your very best, riding your horse with pride, charging your opponent skillfully and hopefully throwing him off his mount."

"I have witnessed several jousting tournaments, papa. I know the rules and realize that I must be strong and alert for the event. Because of my age, however, I have never been allowed to observe a knighting ceremony. What will it be like when my big day comes?"

"The ceremony of knighting, Henri, will be held in the church, right here on the grounds of the Acropolis, when you and several other squires will be directed to appear before the Duke. But the ceremony, will actually have begun the evening before with an all-night prayer vigil before God. At the conclusion of the vigil, you and your comrades will be dressed in white robes symbolic of your promise to be pure and faithful.

"When the big moment comes you will be ushered into the church, one at a time, and in the presence of all knights of the dukedom and the Duke himself you will be asked to dress for battle. You will put on your quilted vest, mail armor over your body, and a hood over your head. Next, you will place your breast plate with the coat of arms of your family clearly visible, steel plates over your knees and arms, and your helmet. The local prelate will present you next with a sword that had been blessed, and you will be asked to kneel in front of the duke. A tap on your shoulder by the duke and you will be a knight!"

"What a charming story, Karyatis! Do you know what happened to Henri? Did he make a good knight?"

"I lost track of him after a while. The word in the fortress was that he was killed in a skirmish in the Peloponnese, defending the last remaining areas there under Frankish control."

In Athens , Sophia, during the years of the Frankish occupation, the local population had become so detached and indidifferent to developments around them, that not even the liberation of Constantinople, from the hands of the hated Crusaders caused a major stir. There was little outward joy when the news reached the city, and suggestions that the event somehow might be the harbinger of a better tomorrow for their city, were dismissed outright.

"Michael Paleologos has reentered Constantinople," I heard a young man bellow one morning, not far from where I was standing. "Emperor Paleologos has retaken Constantinople. Byzantium is free! The Latin rulers are gone. Haghia Sophia is ours again!"

Few persons on the Acropolis that morning responded with visible joy to what should have been blissful news. It was not because of fear of the Franks. For days prior to the announcement, the entire area surrounding the fortress had been devoid of people; the great majority of knights, squires, and foot soldiers, having departed for a military campaign somewhere in Hellas.

"Stop spreading lies, young man," I heard a bystander shout back. "The few Byzantines left in Asia Minor are far too weak to wrest Constantinople away from the Latins."

"It's true! I am not spreading lies, honest I am not," I heard the young man defend himself. "My cousin Neopatris returned last evening on a grain ship from the Black Sea. While crossing the Bosporus and the Sea of Marmara, he and his shipmates observed Byzantine forces guarding the walls of the city. Byzantine forces, not Franks! The colors of emperor Paleologos were flying over the walls of the Imperial city."

"And how did this miracle come about?"inquired the man,

still doubting the auspicious news. "How did Paleologos succeed in expelling the thousands of Latin soldiers from the city, their many ships, and impregnable machines of war?"

"My cousin said, that the ship's captain was so elated at the sight of the liberated Constantinople, that he decided to look around for himself. He dropped anchor off shore in the general vicinity of the Church of Saint George of the Cypresses, and also allowed the crew to disembark. A Thanksgiving service to the *Theotokos* was in progress when the men arrived on the grounds of the church, and hundreds of faithful were waiting patiently outside for the opportunity to enter the jam-packed church.

"From what Neopatris could gather in his talks with those on the grounds of the church, the liberation of the city happened with unbelievable speed and with little if any loss of life.

"It all begun when emperor Paleologos anxious to regain control of the city, that had served as the empire's capital for nearly a thousand years, forged an alliance with Genoa. Under its terms, the Italian port city would help the Byzantine emperor reclaim his capital, in exchange for exclusive trading rights in a free Constantinople. But, before the promised help could arrive from Genoa, an amazing thing happened.

"A Byzantine general, named Alexios Stratigopoulos, leading a small force during a training exercise approached the outer perimeter of Constantinople one evening, when he discovered to his utter amazement that the city was completely undefended. Pausing briefly, Stratigopoulos ordered his men to probe the city walls at different gates. When reports came back that no more than a handful of Frankish soldiers were standing guard at each gate, he ordered the assault. Less than four hours later with the Frankish soldiers running for their lives, the general approached the Iron Gate on the Sea of Marmara. What he saw there truly astonished him. At a nearby wharf, boarding a Venetian ship for the trip back home was the Latin emperor and sovereign of the Kingdom of Constantinople, Baldwin, and his Latin Patriarch! Stratigopoulos made no effort to stop them. After fifty-seven years in the hands of the Franks, Constantinople was his. It was free again.

"The general's first inclination was to dispatch mounted messengers to notify his emperor, and to urge him to rush back to Constantinople to reclaim his capital. Michael Paleologos hesitated at first. How could a few men have breached the impregnable walls and conquered the old city? Could this be a palace coup, or other plot against him?

"But when additional reports confirmed the auspicious news Paleologos returned triumphantly to his capital. Walking alone behind the icon of Panaghia Odigitria, he entered his beloved city at the Golden Gate, to the happy cheers and cries of every one of its citizens. Soon an enormous procession was formed behind him, with the entire population of the city walking slowly in the direction of -- where else? -- but Justinian's Great Church, the Church of Haghia Sophia. Later that evening, as if wanting to reaffirm the city's liberation, Paleologos was crowned Byzantine emperor by the city's new Orthodox Patriarch."

"This is all that was required? A few hundred men to retake Constantinople ? I am wondering, Karyatis, whether

Edward is familiar with the story?"

"If he is not, here's an opportunity for you, Sophia, to show off some of your newly acquired knowledge of history."

"I don't need to do that. Edward and I are comfortable in our careers. He is a historian with a love for teaching, and I am an artist."

"Sounds like you two have a great relationship!"

The liberation of Constantinople, Sophia, and news of an Orthodox Patriarch again ministering to the faithful in the Byzantine capital, made Athenians envious. It reminded them that their own Orthodox prelate had been replaced by a Latin archbishop; in effect, making their church "Latin" and subordinate to Rome.

The "latinization" of the church in Athens had been introduced so rapidly, it had shocked and angered the great majority of the faithful. One of the first acts, for instance, by the Latin Archbishop of Athens was to re-designate the Church of the Panaghia Athiniotissa on the Acropolis, as the Cathedral of Santa Maria. Later, many other Orthodox churches were given Latin names. The Orthodox clergy was similarly "latinized," with bishops and parish priests either being replaced outright with persons loyal to Rome, or allowed to remain in their posts after formally pledging loyalty to the Pope. Latin rites were made mandatory throughout the dukedom, except in some small outlying areas.

All that changed, of course, with the conquest of Hellas by the Ottoman Turks.

I first began hearing of the Turks, Sophia, from a Florentine nobleman by the name of Angelo. Although ostensibly a knight, and bound by oath to the profession of fighting, Angelo did not have it in him to participate in the near continuous military engagements of the period. A banker and money trader by profession, he preferred the leisurely life of Athens, enjoying trips to the countryside or taking long walks with his Athenian wife Antonia and their three children. Their walks would invariably end on the Acropolis and close to my temple.

"I am afraid, Antonia," I heard him whisper to her one afternoon, "our days in Athens are numbered. There is no way that Florence can hang on to the dukedom much longer. Ever since those cursed Catalans engaged the Turks as their confederates in their war against Venice, Hellas has become the battleground for Turkish expansion. Thessaly, Epirus, and parts of the Peloponnese are now firmly under their control, with Thebes expected to fall into their hands soon."

"Are we next?"

"Probably. Technically we are still free, although under the "protection" of the Sultan. How long this arrangement will last is anyone's guess. Rumors are that the Sultan is becoming weary of the mischief by the various Frankish feudal lords, and Byzantine princes, and that he wants to place the city under his military control."

"If that should happen, we'll have to leave?" wondered Antonia.

"Yes. It would mean, of course, separating you from your family in Athens; leaving behind your parents, sister and other relatives. Probably never to see them again."

"Is there a chance, Angelo, that perhaps the Pope, or other political leader in the west might come to our assistance?"

"I doubt it very much, Antonia. Pope Gregory did try a few years back to form a united front against the Turks, and had even convened a meeting of European leaders for that purpose. Everyone able to wield military power in our part of the world was asked to come. The Byzantine emperor attended, as did our own duke, and the leaders of Cyprus, Hungary, and Sicily. Unfortunately, the plans for a collective front collapsed when Turkish troops crushed the Serbs in Kosovo and occupied Serbia.

"The victory encouraged the Turks, and once again they have turned their sights on Hellas. What makes them more dangerous this time, however, is their mastery of the European game of power politics. The Turks will make an "arrangement" with anyone as long as it advances their aims. A few years back, for instance, they allied themselves with Venice against the Byzantines. When that failed to produce the desired results, they switched sides and concluded an agreement with the Orthodox Archbishop of Athens against their former allies the Venetians. Despite their many diplomatic failures and military defeats, the Turks have not given up. Early this year, they returned to Attica again, raiding farmlands, subduing small feudal estates and brutalizing their residents."

"Karyatis, if you don't mind a brief question: Did the final conquest of Athens by the Turks result in much bloodshed?"

"It did. As I recall, general Omar suddenly appeared in Attica early one spring, and despite the lack of organized resistance against him by the Florentines, he ordered the killing, raping, and slaughtering of anyone that his troops would meet on route to Athens.

There was no relief in the carnage, even after the invaders entered the city. Those unable to escape south to the safety of Corinth, which at that time was still under the control of the Byzantines, were attacked and killed brutally. As for the Duke and his retinue, they withdrew into the Acropolis, where they prepared for what they knew was their last chance of defending the Frankish possessions in Hellas.

For two full years, surrounded by a frenzied enemy, and without the help that the authorities back in Florence had promised them, the few remaining Florentines on the Acropolis put up a fierce fight. But so did the Turks. Repeatedly, the enemy succeeded in reaching the defensive perimeter of the Acropolis, only to be repulsed by the combined efforts of every available knight, squire, and foot soldier in the service of the Florentine duke.

I recall those days quite well, Sophia. The ground on the Acropolis shook violently, as the Turkish cannon shells and other war-making machinery at the disposal of general Omar tore large holes on the walls protecting the fortress, at times, even landing amid the defenders in close proximity to the various temples. When the Sultan finally realized that taking the fortress would entail losses far greater than he was prepared to accept, he contacted the Duke. Under an agreement negotiated between the two sides, through the intercession of the abbot of a nearby Orthodox monastery, the Duke of Athens, his family and followers were allowed to depart the Acropolis and seek shelter in the neighboring city of Thebes. There, the Sultan promised, they could live forever free of Turkish interference or control.

The Sultan himself paid a visit to the city soon after, but to everyone's surprise he was not the uncouth barbarian every one had come to fear. Mehmet II was well-read in Hellenic literature, trained in philosophy and was fluent in the language spoken in Hellas. His visit, he announced, was motivated by a desire to pay his respects to a city known for its great past, and contributions to mankind.

During his four-day stay in Athens, the Sultan toured extensively the various landmarks of the city, the Acropolis, and the Orthodox monastery whose abbot earlier had served as the mediator in the negotiations to end the siege. Impressed by everything that he saw, he responded by bestowing upon the city several special favors, including the right of self-government by a council of elderly Athenians. The glorious city of Athens, he declared, would henceforth be administered by its own people, but under the general oversight of the authorities in Constantinople.

The Athenians were not impressed, and soon began maneuvering for the return of the Franks, presumably because they were fellow-Christians. Their unruly plotting forced Mehmet to return to the city; this time, however, at the head of an army. The leaders of the rebellion were imprisoned, and some of the freedoms granted to the city earlier were withdrawn, but Athens escaped more severe punishment.

Life under the Turks was not particularly harsh in Athens. In contrast to the Franks, who coerced the Orthodox faithful to convert to Roman Catholicism, the Turks never pressured anyone to accept Islam as their religion. Orthodox churches and religious property that had been taken over earlier by the Latins were returned to their rightful owners and all positions of authority in the church were filled again with Orthodox clergymen. Free once again to practice their faith, and allowed to run the affairs of their city, Athenians lived peacefully under the Turks; their only obligation to the Sultan being the payment of a tax.

In contrast, conditions on my beloved Acropolis were a lot different. The Acropolis suffered more violence, indignity and horror during the years of Turkish rule, than at any other time in its long history.

Of the numerous indignities committed, none hurt more than the conversion of the Parthenon into a mosque, presumably for use by the Turkish military garrison. The temple of Athena Parthenos, where thousands had prayed through the ages to the Olympian gods, and which later had become a place of worship to the God born in Bethlehem, was now being called upon to serve yet another Almighty. In preparation for this event, the gilded altar serving what was once the Cathedral of Santa Maria was thrown out, Orthodox mosaics were whitewashed, and the remaining Christian symbols were removed or destroyed. Islamic scriptures were added to the interior of the temple, and a tall minaret was erected at the building's southwestern corner. It rose higher than either the statue of Athena Parthenos, or the tower of the former Frankish castle ever did. My own temple did not fare much better. It became the official residence of the local military governor, or Disdar, who proceeded to locate his own harem in the large vestibule, next to where my sisters and I were standing.

Except for the members of the local military garrison and their families, the Acropolis was closed to all persons during the Turkish years. An exception was made for certain foreign visitors who were allowed to enter after payment of a hefty tariff. They were artists, geographers, and historians anxious to check upon and report on the condition of the various temples. But occasionally, opportunists would make their appearance. Under the guise of preparing descriptions of Hellenic works of art for inclusion in literary journals and books, they would remove whatever could be easily carried away, while the Turkish officials (after having been appropriately bribed) looked the other way.

The occasional presence of foreign visitors on the Acropolis, explains why I did not suspect anything evil when the Elgin team under Luisieri first made its appearance. How was I to know that these fellows had ulterior motives? They did not seem different from any of the earlier visitors ; making drawings and examining the various temples was what they all did. It was not until I observed, to my absolute horror, that decorations from the Parthenon were being taken down, that I realized this group was different -- that they were actually thieves!

Venturing into the city during the period of Turkish rule, Sophia, was no longer a joy. The city had changed; it had taken a bland appearance consisting of small unclean homes, many abandoned, or simply vacant. There were few Turks on the streets. Most lived on the Acropolis where they had built homes amid the various temples and along its slopes. I had no difficulty telling the Turks apart. They dressed differently, spoke a strange-sounding language, and their weapons were unlike those that I remembered being carried by Byzantines or Franks. As was their custom, Turkish men wore baggy pants and shirts made of linen or cotton, and covered their heads with a fez or a turban. Women wore a veil as a covering over their face. The more wealthy a person, the more splendid and ornate were his or her clothing. Of the Turks in military uniform, the ones that really stood out for their appearance and discipline, were the members of the elite force known as the janissary. Born mostly into Christian homes, the janissary soldiers were taken away from their families as children, made to convert to Islam, and trained to serve the Sultan with great loyalty and dedication.

Several times in the past, Sophia, after the museum crowds had departed, I found myself wondering: Why did the Turks, who had generally been tolerant, even kindly toward the city of Athens and its citizens, display such intense loathing of the Acropolis? Was it envy for its long and glorious history, or possibly jealousy for the unparalleled beauty of its temples?

What possessed them, for instance, to corrupt the sanctity and physical appearance of the Acropolis by building a myriad of unsightly houses and huts, amid its beautiful temples? Why did they store gunpowder inside the Parthenon at a time when the city was coming under fire by the Venetians? Were these stupid errors by low ranking Turkish officials, or possibly conscious decisions by people who hated everything reminiscent of the glory that once was Hellas?

The madman Morosini is intimately connected with the episode of the explosion of the stored gunpowder inside the Parthenon. Several days after the event, with much of the temple still in ruins, he appeared on the Acropolis totally obsessed with himself. He was proud of having expelled the Turks from the city, but as far as I could tell, there was not a speck of regret or remorse for his horrendous crime.

"How was I to know, that the Turks had stored gunpowder in the temple?" I heard him ask casually a member of his entourage. "I did not find out about it, until one of our mortar bombs hit the temple and debris from the building flew over to our camp."

It was a lie, Sophia! Morosini knew quite well that the Parthenon was being used by the Turks to store explosives, and also that it was being used by senior Turkish officials as a shelter. A Turkish deserter had told him so. The Ottoman authorities, he had reported to Morosini are convinced that the Venetians would never attack the temple out of respect for its history.

It was not until Morosini approached the Parthenon itself, that he realized the enormity of the damage that the Turkish action and his own folly had caused. The roof of the temple lay on the ground, the wall of the cella, and many of the columns had collapsed, and a major part of the frieze had been shattered by the explosion. What had been left of the explosives continued to burn for another day or two.

"Look," he added defensively. "My original orders from Venice were to wrestle the Peloponnese and Evia, away from the Turks. The Peloponnese and Evia, nothing more! Don't venture into Attica, I had been warned. Stay away from the rest of the Hellenic mainland.

"But the people of Athens would hear none of it. We had barely liberated Corinth, and Nafplion, when their delegates showed up at my tent, appealing with me to come save their city from the oppressors. Free us from the rule of the Muslims, they pleaded. We are Christians, like you, who deserve protection. Their appeals became so numerous and intense, I finally gave in. I loaded nine hundred horses and eight thousand men on our ships, and set sail for the port of Piraeus.

"The Turks reacted instantly, evacuating the lower city and assembling all their forces on the Acropolis. Expecting an assault from the direction of Piraeus, they proceeded to place their heaviest guns at the Propylaea.

"What could I do? Repeatedly, I offered them the opportunity to surrender, but they would not hear of it. So I ordered the placement of our guns on the hills opposite theirs, and opened fire.

"At first our bombardment either hit the Acropolis walls or flew over their target into the city below -- in effect doing no damage to the defending Turks. It was then, that my artillery officer Muttoni who was leading the barrage suggested that we move our guns closer to the Acropolis. I agreed, which led to the unfortunate hit on the Parthenon. I hear that along with the temple many Turkish homes burned, and three hundred defenders were killed, including the Turkish commandant and his son. The Turks surrendered soon thereafter."

"Did the Venetians remain long in Athens?"

"No. No more than a year. They had never intended to occupy the city anyway. When a strange illness began affecting their troops in the Peloponnese, they withdrew their forces from the city, and the Turks returned. As they were departing, Morosini and his men loaded their boats with numerous pieces of Hellenic art, not unlike many earlier conquerors of the city."

X

THE FIRMAN

Sophia and Edward's fourth anniversary celebration was a departure from the usual. Concerned that their long separation, because of his sabbatical in Washington, might have adversely affected their relationship, Edward surprised her with a plan for the evening's entertainment that promised to be enjoyable, and a lot more lavish than usual. Their evening, he announced on arriving at her studio carrying a large bouquet of red roses, would start with a visit to Covent Garden for a performance of her beloved Verdi opera of *Don Carlo.* It would continue with a candlelight dinner at an intimate restaurant just off Piccadilly, and conclude with dancing and after-dinner drinks at the penthouse of the newest London club overlooking Trafalgar Square and its stunning Christmas tree.

The words coming from Edward, who was not known for being particularly imaginative or adventurous when planning their social events, left Sophia speechless.

"We'd better hurry, dear," he urged her. "The limousine is

parked illegally and we do not want to miss the opening act of *Carlo*."

Although by nature not a suspicious person, the evening's plans and the excess of it all left Sophia wondering. A limousine? Opera? Dancing at a new London club? What was Edward up to? It was all so very unlike their customary dinner and concert routine of the past four years.

Had she possibly said something inadvertently to him, that had made him fearful of losing her? Had Edward perhaps strayed into another woman's arms while in Washington, and was now attempting to conceal the affair with a dazzling evening out?

Thoughts of her own feelings toward Edward absorbed Sophia during the short ride to Covent Garden, and also as she sat quietly next to him through the first act of *Carlo*. But soon, the exquisite arias of Verdi's grand opera and the drama of the young prince still in love with his former fiancée, a French princess who was now married to his father the king, overtook her thoughts. Edward is a good man, she concluded. We are fortunate to have each other.

True to promise, the restaurant selected by Edward for the evening's meal was a gourmet's heaven. Its kitchen was in the hands of a master chef, whose selections though not exactly standard English fare made him unique in London for culinary accomplishment. Intimate and small, it was also a jewel of virtual art, with every bit of its wall space decorated with works of aspiring young artists, including statuettes and figurines of a caliber normally seen in museums.

Over dessert of fresh strawberries, immersed in whipped cream and cognac, Edward asked her.

"How is the Caryatid portrait coming along?"

"I still have quite a bit of work to do. She is so very beautiful, Ed, I sure hope that I'll do her justice."

"Of course you will."

"She is really difficult to do. As you know, I like to immerse myself in a subject before attempting to represent it on canvas. But in the case of the Caryatid, this process is turning out to be a lot more complex."

"In what way?"

"Hard to explain. From the very outset, I have been intrigued by her facial expression and the way her eyes are staring at me. She appears to be proud and full of youthful joy, yet also sad, which is reflective perhaps of the mood that her maker was in when he gave her life over two thousand years ago. She was done, you know, during a period of great stress, during the long and bitter conflict between Athens and Sparta.

"Perhaps, his life was sad and dispirited -- shaped by wars and invasions -- and unconsciously, he allowed it to be reflected on his subject.

"This uncertainty about her, Edward, has awakened in me a deep desire to learn all I can about her, from the moment she took her place on the Erechtheum along with her sisters, to the time she arrived to our shores. With you in Washington, I have been doing a lot of reading on her, and… strange as it might sound, … I have ended up developing a kind of personal attachment to her.

"She's quite a girl, you know, with a fantastic tale: her many years on the Acropolis; being witness to more civilizations and empires that most people have even heard about; to her abduction and transportation to London."

Sophia had hardly finished her last sentence, when she realized that this was neither the place nor the time for a discussion of a controversial subject, one on which she and Edward most likely were holding differing points of view.

"And how are things at the university?" she inquired, clearly in an effort to change the subject.

"Slowly catching up," he answered casually. "I am behind schedule, though, on some of my museum activities. The students' demonstration the other day, has only added to my workload. Apparently, two students who had been particularly rowdy were being hand-cuffed by the police at the precise moment that the wife of the American Vice-President was entering the building. They tell me, that she was really troubled by what she saw and once inside Duveen Gallery, and beyond the reporters ears, began asking questions that were clearly supportive of the students' point of view."

"You mean, the reasons why the museum is still holding on to the Parthenon sculptures?"

"Yes. Unfortunately, a local paper in London and another one in Scotland, have since picked up the same theme, accusing the police of brutality toward the students and questioning our legal right to the sculptures. I really think that foreign interests were orchestrating this entire protest."

"I did read the editorial in the London paper this morning, Edward."

"So did I. And, judging from its language it might as well have been written in Athens. I just don't understand the Greeks, Sophia. We rescued their art from certain destruction and now they are accusing us of having stolen it? As a result of this mess, a special meeting of the Museum's Board has been scheduled for Friday afternoon. I don't know what it will accomplish. The Board has ruled repeatedly on this issue."

"It has?"

"Yes. The Parthenon sculptures are here to stay. Case closed!"

Edward's words were ringing in Sophia's ears the next morning as she was going through her daily routine, and also during the short walk to her health spa for her workout. She had suspected all along that Edward would adhere to the museum's line on the issue of the sculptures, but the inflexibility of his position had taken her aback. Why did he have to use the words "case closed?" They sounded so final!

How could she explain to her friend, the Karyatis, that Edward whom she was anxiously waiting to meet, and for whom she appeared to have positive feelings, was among those responsible for her continued captivity in London? Would she want to continue with her story, or would anger overtake her and cause an end to their unique but also puzzling relationship?

Though still quite a distance away, patiently waiting for the large museum crowd to wind its way through the Great Hall and into the Caryatid's room, Sophia could already feel her vibrations.

"You are late, my friend. It must have been quite an evening! Did everything turn out as you had expected?"

"Sure did. Edward really outdid himself this time. We began at the opera, had an exquisite dinner at an intimate restaurant, and concluded our evening in London's latest night club dancing to the tunes of a dreamy 1940s band. It was all very beautiful; truly a charming evening, and a fitting celebration of our four years together."

"I am happy for you, Sophia."

"Thank you. But, it's back to work for me, Karyatis. The magazine doing the story on my art show wants to include a photo of your portrait. I'll have to have it ready in two weeks."

"You will be able to continue with my story, won't you. Your earlier account of Elgin has really peaked my curiosity. From my location, other than seeing the members of his team move about, I had no way of knowing what went on behind the scenes."

A lot of things were going on behind the scenes. As you recall, Karyatis, from our earlier discussion, while Elgin sailed to his post in Constantinople, the team under Lusieri that had been charged with preparing drawings and casts of ancient art arrived in Athens. The local Disdar, or military governor, initially granted the team permission to begin its work on payment of the customary fee of five guineas per day per worker. But, when the magnitude of the team's effort became apparent, especially its plan to prepare casts of major pieces or art, he had a change of heart. No further work could be accomplished, he announced, without permission or a "firman" from Constantinople.

Lusieri, already greatly annoyed with the Disdar for not allowing him to erect scaffolding with which to examine the frieze of the Parthenon, and the upper sections of the other temples on the Acropolis, rushed to Constantinople. The Disdar is forever getting in our way, he advised Elgin, and work cannot progress with him dissenting to our every request. What was needed was a firman, issued at the highest levels of the Ottoman government, that will remove the military governor from the chain of command, and allow work to resume without his interference.

A similar plea to Elgin was made by Dr. Philip Hunt. You recall him? He was the Embassy chaplain who eventually convinced Elgin of the need to "rescue" the art on the Acropolis. A firman, he also advised the ambassador, was essential so the team could enter the Acropolis freely, erect the necessary scaffolding, and make drawings and plaster models of ancient temples. But, the firman should also allow the team - in Hunt's words –"*to remove any sculptures or inscriptions which do not interfere with the works or walls of the citadel.*"

Had Elgin still intended to merely make drawings of the ancient monuments, and plaster casts of the more interesting ones (which had been his original plan), he would have most certainly vetoed Dr. Hunt's proposal, especially the one about removing sculptures or inscriptions. By the time, however, that the firman issue had surfaced, Elgin's outlook toward the entire matter of copying Hellenic art for his architect and the people back home was undergoing a major change.

Elgin had come under the influence of Dr. Hunt, who would return from his travels to Athens full of gloomy descriptions of the deteriorating conditions of the art treasures on the Acropolis. Then, there was also the matter of the mansion in Scotland, whose interior décor was beginning to preoccupy Elgin. A letter exists in which he lists the various decorative items for the mansion, that Lusieri should procure for him. It included examples of a frieze, a capital from a column, a metope, as well as individual columns for adorning the main hall of the mansion.

It was hardly surprising then, that Elgin's application to the Sublime Porte -- the government in Constantinople -- would follow Dr. Hunt's recommendation, and request that the team be allowed *to remove some pieces of stone with old inscriptions or figures thereon.*

At this point, we can only speculate. What did the words *some pieces of stone* really mean? Pieces of sculptures that had fallen on the ground, or the many statues that Elgin ultimately removed? One thing is clear: Elgin did not request the right to remove complete sculptures, but neither did he preclude that possibility either. Perhaps, he was intentionally vague with respect to what he had in mind.

When the firman was finally issued, it allowed the team to make drawings and casts of the sculptures in place, and to excavate around the buildings. But it also commanded the authorities in Athens not to meddle with the scaffolding and other implements of the team, nor to hinder *their taking away any pieces of stone (qualche pezzi di pietra) with inscriptions or figures.* Signed by the Acting Grand Vizir, the firman placed only one prohibition on the team -- not to damage the monuments themselves while doing their work.

It is around the language of the firman, Karyatis, that much of the controversy surrounding Lord Elgin's removal of the sculptures revolves. If the application for the firman had been vague, the firman itself was even more so. What did it allow Elgin's team to remove? *Pieces of stone with inscriptions* only, or any marble sculpture on the Acropolis that Lusieri and company happened to take a liking to? Did it apply to the Parthenon only, or to all other temples on the Acropolis?

It is impossible to know for sure. The original firman no longer exists and an Italian translation that is available fails to answer these questions authoritatively.

"I hate to interrupt you, Sophia, but two questions come to mind: As far back as I can recall, the Ottoman authorities were highly protective of the Acropolis. It was after all their military citadel. Very few visitors if any were allowed to enter the grounds, and the few that were given access were extremely restricted in what they could do during their stay. Why then, were the Ottomans all of a sudden so very generous toward Elgin and in effect allowed his team to plunder the Acropolis?

"Also, the way you have presented the story thus far, it almost makes it appear as if the decision to raid the Parthenon was driven by Dr. Hunt, was made possible by a vague Turkish firman, with Lord Elgin merely going along. If that is the case, why is everyone placing so much blame on Elgin? The Turks and Dr. Hunt share equal responsibility."

"Good questions, Karyatis, both of them".

With regard to the Ottomans' generosity toward Elgin: By any measure, Elgin was extremely lucky in that he arrived in Constantinople at a time that events were drawing Turkey into an alliance with Britain, causing the Sultan to be extremely accommodating to the British Ambassador. When Elgin asked the Sultan for a firman, Lord Nelson had just fought and won the battle of the Nile, the French Army had capitulated to the British, and the balance of power in the eastern Mediterranean had been radically altered. It was this coincidence of circumstances, that made it possible for Lord Elgin to exploit his position as ambassador in His Majesty's service, and seek successfully the favors that he wanted.

Regarding your second question: Even with the passage of time, it is still impossible to know for sure who was responsible for the order which allowed the removal of the sculptures from the Parthenon. Years later, when Dr. Hunt was questioned, he blamed the Turks for issuing the vague firman, and for not rejecting Lusieri's initial request to take down a metope. But, if the firman pertained to the Parthenon only, why did Luisieri and company remove you from your temple, and also the column that now stands across from you in the museum?

My personal view, Karyatis, is that the decision to raid the Parthenon was made by Elgin with Lusieri acting as his agent. The authority had to be Elgin's; he was paying the bills after all, and Lusieri was accountable to him. The suggestion that Elgin somehow went along with the idea, when he later visited Athens and after learning that the Turks had been destroying sculptures on the Acropolis to produce mortar for the construction of their homes, does not hold. The removal of the Parthenon sculptures and their packing for their trip to London, had begun at least six months *before* Elgin's one and only visit to the site in Athens. The team in Athens, and Elgin, must have been in full agreement on the scope of the work from the very beginning. Evidence also the fact that early on in the process, Lusieri asked Elgin to provide him with marble saws of various sizes, which Elgin rushed to him without delay. Why would Lusieri need marble saws if not to take down sculptures? And why would Elgin respond to that request, unless he was part of the illicit work plan for the removal of the sculptures?

The firman, Karyatis, was hand carried to Athens by Dr. Hunt, and immediately Lusieri ordered his men to begin erecting the scaffolding around the Parthenon. From your location you must have been able to observe the workmen fastening the pillars and other support props, necessary to reach the upper sections of the temple.

What you could not have been aware of was, that at about the same time Lusieri was meeting with the Voivode seeking from him permission to bring down one of the metopes of the Parthenon -- presumably, on the authority granted in the firman. The Turkish official wasn't about to overrule the Acting Great Vizir's directive, so he routinely approved the request. Anyone else, of course, would have pointed out to Lusieri, that the Vizir's directive said nothing of taking down entire pieces of sculpture such as the removal of the metope entailed.

"I can certainly recall the day, Sophia, when the scaffolding began to go up. At first, I had no reason to be concerned; a bit puzzled, yes; but concerned, no. I wondered what the Turks were up to. Are they possibly planning to repair the damage to the temple suffered in Morosini's bombing?

"But I pained... hurt deep down, when I realized belatedly, what the entire operation was all about. The sight of the first metope coming down literally devastated me."

The work of stripping the Parthenon of its finest treasures lasted a long time, Sophia. and since I was among the last statues to go, I was able to observe most of the work. Behaving at times like thugs, Elgin's men numbering at times more than a hundred, took down sculptures that had been in place for centuries, carelessly smashing many pieces in the process, and ravaging the temple of its architectural unity and beauty. By the time I was gone, they had removed the very best that the Parthenon had to offer. The damage to the temple and its sculptures had been enormous.

Careless handling by Lusieri's men caused much damage. Repeatedly, sculptures and other pieces of marble would come crashing down, for no apparent reason other than lack of attention on the part of the workmen. The most serious damage, however, occurred during the team's attempts to separate the metopes from the outside frieze of the temple. The metopes, sandwiched between triglyphs, could not be detached from their location until the cornices above them had been separated, and the entablature on which they rested destroyed. The cornices rarely survived the separation, with Lusieri's men simply allowing them, inexcusably, to fall to the ground. Serious damage to the temple was caused also, during the process of removing sections of the frieze and of many pediment structures. To reduce the weight of the removed frieze slabs, and ease their weight for the trip to England, Lusieri did not hesitate to order the sawing off and discarding of large parts of the marble sculpture.

I knew that I would be next, Sophia, when Dr. Hunt suddenly appeared in front of my temple one morning. Seeing him on the Acropolis was always bad news, but on that particular day his presence conveyed an especially ominous message to me. His usual jovial mood was missing, and his face depicted deep anxiety. He was obviously struggling with a very serious problem, which explained also why he had skipped his customary walk that morning.

I recall thinking: this cannot be a casual visit; whatever he is up to, it's got to be bad. Why else would he just be sitting there, for hours on, staring at my sisters and me?

Lusieri arrived soon with some of the same men that I had seen before working on the pediment of the Parthenon. They were carrying their usual tools, which naturally increased my anxiety.

Dr. Hunt and Lusieri lost no time becoming engulfed in an ugly argument. I could not make out the particulars, but their body language and finger pointing convinced me that something pertaining to my temple was at issue.

"We can only go with one," I heard Lurieri's voice rising above the debate. "There is no way that we can find a ship large enough to transport the entire portico. Let's begin with that one," he added, pointing his fearsome finger at me.

"Won't you please wait at least until we hear from the admiral," pleaded Hunt.

"No. We've got to move on," answered Lusieri, rudely. "We simply cannot wait for him. His Lordship has been very explicit to me on this. He wants no more delays." With these words Lusieri turned in the direction of the two Turkish men standing behind him.

"Go," he directed. "Take her down!"

Seeing those huge ugly saws, Sophia, advancing toward me almost made me feel faint.

"Go away," I began screaming, "don't touch me!" But to no avail. Within minutes four huge men had separated me from my temple, while many others nearby struggled to keep me upright. I could hear the slow grinding noise of the saws throughout the entire operation.

"Bring her down, carefully," warned Lusieri in a booming voice. "We don't want anything happening to her! And when you are done, build a brick pillar in her place, to hold the portico steady."

By the time I was lowered into what felt like a wooden container, I was totally overcome with fear. Having observed the Turks in the past picking up pieces of marble that had fallen on the ground and crushing them to produce mortar, I had no idea what to expect next. Is this what was likely to happen to me too?

I lost track of time over the next several days. Stuffed in a box, I kept waiting for Lusieri's next move. One thing I was certain of: I was still near my temple for I could feel the presence of my sisters nearby. And after all those years of total silence on their part -- as strange as it might sound now -- I could hear them suddenly fill the air every evening with the most mournful sighs and lamentations for me. I tried responding in kind, but I will never know whether they heard me.

As for my last day on the Acropolis, Sophia, I don't think that I'll be able ever to forget it. For days I would hear talk from the workers, about this large shiny man of war in the service of Admiral Nelson that had arrived in the port of Piraeus. Lusieri, the men reported ,was preparing a list of the cases that would be selected for the trip to Britain.

"Britain?" I wondered. "Where is that? Where are they taking me?"

Apparently, I was one of the statues identified to go. Early one morning three men showed up; after closing my case tightly, and banging on it without mercy, they pronounced it safe for the trip. A cart pulled up next to me, and I was off -- off to a strange land that I had no desire of being.

"Will you fill in details on the rest of my story, Sophia, from that point on?"

"Yes. But first, let me mention an incident that occurred soon after you were removed from your temple. Do you recall Lusieri ordering his men to erect a brick pillar where you were standing, in order to support the portico and prevent it from coming down? Well? They did build a crude sort of pillar, which they positioned dutifully at the very spot that you used to occupy. Next to your beautiful sisters, the thing was very, very ugly, which prompted Lord Byron when he visited the Acropolis later to scribble on it the words "Opus Elgin," meaning "Done by Elgin."

The Elgin operation, Karyatis, netted a total of 90 pieces of unrivaled art, including 56 panels of the Parthenon frieze, 15 metopes, 17 statues from the east and west pediments, an Ionian column from your own temple the Erechtheum, and of course you. All pieces except for you, and the Ionian column are exhibited next door in the Duveen Gallery. Throughout it all, Lusieri remained in charge. Elgin came down only once but he continued to orchestrate the effort from Constantinople. Regularly he would pressure Lusieri to move on with greater speed, citing the possibility that the Sultan might switch sides, drop the British, and again become friends with the French. The loot itself was packed in hundreds of cases and shipped here to Britain over a period of several years. The transportation was mostly on British naval ships that were operating in the Mediterranean, like the one you came on. All did not go well, however. Some shipments experienced mishaps, as was the case of the *Mentor* that had been purchased by Elgin for the express purpose of transporting the sculptures to Britain.

On its maiden voyage in the service of Elgin, the *Mentor* left Piraeus with seventeen boxes of molds and sculptures including a piece of the Parthenon frieze. Near the island of Kythera, however, the ship encountered a bad storm and sank in deep water. Its freight was not recovered until four years later, at an extreme cost to Elgin.

There is an interesting anecdote, Karyatis, in connection with the *Mentor*. It appears that during the efforts to recover the lost treasure Elgin contacted the British consul in Kythera to request his help. When the latter inquired on the nature of the shipment, Elgin reportedly answered: "Nothing very important, merely seventeen cases of stones of no great value." Can you believe that? Stones of no great value?

With his treasures safely packed and awaiting shipment in Piraeus, Elgin decided to return home. While on route, however, war broke out between Britain and France and he was arrested by the French, and held prisoner by them for three years. These were not good times for Elgin. His wife Mary had left him for another man, and his health had deteriorated. By the time he returned home most cases containing his marbles had arrived, but it took another five years for everything to get there. As for Lusieri, he remained in Athens for a while longer. But once all crates had been shipped to London, Elgin let him go. Lusieri died in Athens a few years later.

You are probably wondering why the French let Elgin go? They tried hard to acquire his Parthenon loot themselves, and for a while they even threatened to keep him in jail until he sold the sculptures to them. But Elgin refused. Thus, at the end of this entire adventure he could claim that he had met at least one of his original goals, that of bringing the Parthenon treasures to London, and introducing them to the people of Britain.

XI

THE PARTHENON SCULPTURES IN LONDON

The arrival in London of Elgin and of his loot were met with mixed reaction by the art circles of Britain. It was not unusual, Karyatis, for Elgin to be greeted at public appearances with cries of "plunderer!" and "pilferer!" Granted, charged his critics, the Parthenon had been damaged by wars and neglect, but was that sufficient justification to rape the most beautiful building in the world? Elgin's admirers were equally outspoken. Elgin, they countered, did what any prudent man would have done under similar circumstances. The Acropolis art was doomed and he acted to rescue it.

"They could not have been serious, Sophia."

"It is true, and let me mention a fact that you probably are not aware of: To this very day there is a divergence of views with regard to Elgin's actions. Millions consider him a thief of the worst kind, but many others believe that he is being unjustly defamed for having the courage and foresight to do a noble act."

"Stealing a hundred pieces of art from the Acropolis was a noble act?"

"I feel as you do, but it seems that many others don't. No use belaboring the point now. We need to go on with our story.

"Do you have any recollections of your first years in London, Karyatis?"

"Not many!

"Until our arrival in the British Museum, Sophia, London felt like the worst kind of prison. First were the years when we were shuffled from one storage area to another, while ...His Lordship tried to decide what to do with us. The maltreatment that we suffered amid London's damp climate and the uncertainty of it all was dreadful.

"Then came that awful exercise in ignorance, when the British Museum prior to moving us to its newly built Duveen Gallery decided to enhance the appearance of most sculptures by making them "more white" than they were, if you can believe that. Personally, I was not exposed to that indignity, but many others were.

"Finally, there were the years of World War II and the bombing of the city of London that necessitated yet another move, this time however for our safety.

"This is basically about all that I can recall, Sophia."

"In that case, let me fill in with what I have gathered from my readings."

Elgin had hardly been freed by the French when he arrived in London in search of his collection. The majority of the cases it turned out had already been delivered and were being kept unopened at various places in the city, including the London Customs House. In desperate need financially, and anxious to begin publicizing his collection for the purpose of securing a buyer, Elgin lost no time in obtaining access to his valuable spoils and also leasing a property for their temporary storage. The site selected, on Park Lane and Piccadilly in the center of London, included an empty lot where Elgin decided to erect a large building for use as a gallery for his collection. It is probably one of the sites that you may recall, Karyatis.

By the time Elgin had become settled in London, he had abandoned his earlier plan of using the Parthenon art for decorating his mansion in Scotland. His wife for whom the mansion had been intended had left him. She had taken advantage of his absence in France to live openly with another man, a neighbor, whom she later married. With the Scottish mansion no longer an issue, Elgin turned his attention to either establishing a permanent museum in London for exhibiting the treasures for profit -- a frightfully expensive proposition to be sure -- or that failing, for the sale of the entire collection to the British government.

While Elgin pondered his two options, the storage of the art again became a problem when the house on Park Lane was sold and he was asked to vacate the premises. Through the intercession of a friend, Elgin was successful in locating another London location, this time on the grounds of the Burlington House. But he could not afford the cost of erecting another gallery so you and the others, Karyatis, ended up being kept in an outside shed normally used for coal storage. Because of his absence in Constantinople and later in France,

Elgin had not actually had the opportunity to view his entire collection until he had it moved to the property on Park Lane. Seeing the sculptures for the first time, he was thunderstruck by their beauty. Immediately he sought out the most important art critics and dealers of Britain, and several of them came calling to his gallery to admire his bounty, including Prince Ludwig of Bavaria known for his hunger of fine art. Among the visitors was also an Italian artist by the name of Canova, whom Elgin requested to "restore" the Parthenon sculptures for him.

"Restore" them, Canova asked in obvious horror? "How can I or any other man touch these sculptures with a chisel? They are the work of the greatest artists the world has ever seen."

Despite the universal acclaim that surrounded his collection, Elgin realized before too long that his limited finances could not support the opening of a private museum. Selling the collection, therefore, to the British government became his only viable option. The urgency to sell received a further impetus, when the Burlington House where the art was being housed was sold and Elgin once again was asked to leave.

Elgin began sounding out friends within the government. Would His Majesty's government be amenable to purchasing the collection, he inquired? Among others, he contacted the Paymaster-General. He was prepared to transfer the ownership of his collection to the government he told him, for the price of £ 62,000. The offer was ignored, but unofficially Elgin was advised that the most the government was prepared to pay was £ 30,000.

By the time that Elgin agreed to offer his art to the government, which he did by means of a formal letter to the Chancellor of the Exchequer, he had raised its price to £ 74,000. This figure, he claimed included all expenses incurred up to that date, including the hiring of artists, removing the art from the Parthenon, transporting it to Britain, expenses in London, and also £ 23,000 in interest that he would have accrued had he used his funds in another business venture. In his letter to the Chancellor of the Exchequer, Elgin suggested, that in the event that his offer was refused a committee of the House of Commons be established to determine the final value of the collection. He would then abide by its decision.

The Chancellor agreed -- not with the requested price of course -- but with the suggestion that the entire question be referred to a Committee of the House of Commons. When it was finally established, the Parliamentary Committee offered Elgin no more than £ 35,000. Many of its members argued, that the sculptures had been acquired while he was a public servant and he had borne few if any transportation expenses -- the majority of the items having been transported to London by British warships. Still, the Parliamentary Committee found that "the collection had been legitimately acquired by Elgin as a private individual, " and offered him what it felt was a fair price. Elgin's finances at that time were so bad he accepted the figure with a minimum of moaning. Eventually, an Act of Parliament transferred the ownership of the Parthenon collection to the British nation and vested its safekeeping to the trustees of the British Museum "in perpetuity."

"Do these words imply, Sophia, that I can never be returned to my homeland? Ever?"

"I am afraid it will require another Act of Parliament before you and the other pieces of the Parthenon collection are allowed to leave. Under legislation passed a number of years ago, the museum trustees are prohibited from disposing of objects unless duplicates are already in the collection, which in your case of course there are none."

"Your friend Edward is a trustee. He can help, perhaps?"

"Yes, but he's only one of several. Under certain conditions the trustees are authorized to make loans of the museum's holdings for public exhibition elsewhere. But, they are prohibited from making permanent transfers."

"If I understand you then, Sophia, I can only be returned to the Acropolis as part of a loan arrangement of some kind?"

"I am afraid so, or unless Parliament rules differently."

"I cannot believe it!"

"Oh be fair, Karyatis. You, and the Parthenon collection, have been treated well by the British Museum. You are being exhibited in Britain's largest museum, one of the world's oldest I might add. The museum is London's most visited tourist attraction, and more than six million people stop by annually to delight in its holdings, free of charge. This is a huge number of visitors by any standard. As for the Duveen Gallery where the majority of the Acropolis art is physically located, it certainly is as elegant a museum home as any. Thousands of other works of art languish in substandard buildings, all over the world."

"But, we've not always been here, Sophia. For a very long time we were housed in very modest temporary galleries."

"I know that. The opening of Duveen was delayed by the threat of the war in Europe, Karyatis. But, when the fighting began the authorities did their best to look after you. A lot better, probably, than your sisters were looked after on the Acropolis."

"I don't know what happened to them during the war, but as for me, I recall being moved to a deep site in an underground station, along with several pediment figures and metopes from the temple. We spent the war years in this cold and damp site surrounded by dozens of large sand bags. It wasn't pleasant at all."

"You were evacuated just in time, Karyatis, because soon afterward the bombing of the city began. The Duveen Gallery, incidentally, was one of the buildings that was severely damaged by the bombing. You could have been destroyed!"

"I could hear the sirens wailing and the noise from the bombs dropping on the city, in the neighborhood where I was being kept."

"I am not surprised. Hundreds of planes blasted London almost continuously for two months. Fires consumed entire sections of the city, and people sought shelter wherever they could. I recall Edward's mother telling me, that she spent the entire period of the 'German blitz' deep in an underground shelter underneath her local church."

I asked you earlier, Karyatis, to be fair toward the British Museum. Now, it is my turn to be fair.

The museum certainly deserves high marks for its stewardship of the Parthenon sculptures, for sheltering them from damage during the war, and for exhibiting them in a state-of-the art facility. But the museum is also responsible for having damaged the sculptures, perhaps irreparably, during their absurd effort a few years back to have them "cleaned."

You recall the event. It began with Lord Duveen offering to donate a new gallery to the British Museum for housing the Parthenon sculptures. The honeyed color of the statues, he complained to the museum curators, would not look right in the new gallery. Why not undertake a conservation project to make the statues… "whiter," as they had presumably been on the Parthenon? Lord Duveen, incidentally, was an art dealer known for "cleaning up" paintings of the Old Masters so that they could bring a higher price by wealthy art collectors.

You, Karyatis, more so than anyone else should know that the Pentelic marble from which the Parthenon statues had been sculpted, though brilliant white in color, has the characteristic of appearing a soft yellow under certain light conditions. It was this soft yellow shade that Duveen asked to be "cleaned" away!

The museum responded positively to the suggestion of its benefactor. But, instead of the customary soap and water used for cleaning the marble, copper chisels, hard-wire brushes, and some very strong chemicals were used. Two years later when the generally unsupervised cleaning crew was done, complaints began pouring in. Many of the marbles suddenly appeared white! An internal investigation followed which led to the discharge or early retirement of those responsible. But, the damage had already been done.

The Greek government, which has been pressing Britain to return the Parthenon sculptures to Athens, is very critical of the episode. The "cleaning," it charges, has inflicted irreparable damage on the collection. Scrubbing the marbles with chisels and hard-wire brushes, has removed the patina and has stripped them much of their original detail.

"How are the museum authorities reacting to the Greek charges?"

"They are not denying that the heavy-handed cleaning performed by the museum staff was wrong -- in fact some very important museum people have referred to this incident as a scandal -- but they reject the accusations by the Greek side of heavy damage having been made. The Greeks, they charge, are exaggerating the damage to the sculptures for political purposes. The loss of surface in most cases is barely visible, and millions have viewed the marbles without noticing the difference. Besides, the museum points out the mistake happened sixty years ago, implying that it is all water over the dam!"

"Did any sculptures survive the cleaning unscathed, Sophia?"

"A few did, and remarkably, they all were sculptures of gods."

"Of gods? It pleases me no end! This should finally put an end to all the silly talk of the Olympian gods being dead. What better proof is needed that they are alive and well?"

To conclude our discussion of Elgin, Karyatis: He and his team removed a total of ninety individual large pieces of art from the Acropolis. Not just *pieces of stone,* that the Ottoman firman said that could be removed, but ninety *large sculptures of unique art,* including your own statue and one column from your temple. The art is housed now in this building, and collectively represents about half of all sculpture that originally adorned the Parthenon. The remainder is in Athens, of course, in the new Acropolis Museum.

To its credit, the Duveen Gallery which incidentally is rectangular in shape as is the Parthenon, has made every effort to display the art in the same location it once occupied on the original monument. Thus, the seventeen sculptures removed from the Parthenon's east and west pediments, are exhibited at the two ends of the gallery and in the approximate location and relationship to each other, as on the original pediments. Displayed nearby are the fifteen metopes that were removed from the outer frieze of the temple. The fifty-six panels of the frieze that originally adorned the Parthenon's cella, are positioned at Duveen along the gallery's two long walls.

The statues on the east pediment, you recall, once depicted the birth of the goddess Athena. There were fourteen statues on the original pediment, and of these ten have found their way here, courtesy of Mr. Elgin. My favorite one is the twin statue of Demeter and her daughter Persephone. A true master must have chiseled them out of the same block of marble. The two goddesses are shown together in an elegant pose, and even though their heads are missing, they seem to be gazing in the direction of Zeus. Goddess Athena is standing erect in the center of the pediment.

Of the original art on the west pediment, four complete statues and parts of six others can be seen here. The theme of the west décor was the fight between goddess Athena and Poseidon for the patronage of the city of Athens, which of course she won. Included in the exhibit is a part of the original statue of Athena, the entire torso of Hermes, and a fairly complete statue of Iris the messenger of the gods. My favorite is a beautiful male figure named after Kephissos the river that runs through Athens. He is shown reclining, but unfortunately his head and arms are also missing.

Originally there were ninety-two metopes on the Parthenon, thirty-two on each long side and fourteen at each end. The metopes were placed around the building above the row of outside columns, each metope being separated from its neighbors by a decoration known as a triglyph. Elgin and company helped themselves to fifteen of the metopes, and since they were all taken from the same side of the Parthenon, they all depict scenes with the same theme -- the struggle between the Lapiths and the Centaurs. I recall mentioning the story earlier, of the Centaurs visiting the kingdom of the Lapiths, becoming drunk at a wedding, and then trying to make off with the Lapith women. The fight that ensued is depicted on the metopes held by the museum.

The fifty-six panels that originally adorned the frieze of the Parthenon's inner temple, or cella, depict hundreds of human figures and animals moving in a continuous procession at the time of the Panathenaea festival. There are dozens of outstanding panels in the collection. The ones that I like to point out to my friends, when touring the gallery, depict the ceremony of the presentation of the sacred *peplos* or robe to the goddess Athena. A priest and a young boy are holding the *peplos,* and three maidens carrying ceremonial objects on their heads walk solemnly toward the temple. Hermes, the messenger of the gods is shown looking in the direction of the procession. Leaning on his shoulder is Dionysios, the god of wine. Demeter and Ares, the god of war, are seated nearby. On an unusually long panel is Zeus, the father of the gods, recognized by his scepter and throne. His wife, Hera, is next to him and by her side stands Iris, a messenger deity.

"I have a feeling that you are done, Sophia."

"Yes. This is basically the story of the man, Karyatis. What can I say? He was an opportunist who, with the Turks looking the other way stripped the Parthenon clean of much of its art. I am sorry you ended up being one of his victims."

"What seems unbelievable to me is that he is gotten away with it.

"Before you go, Sophia, I am curious: what has happened to the Acropolis since I've gone? And, what about my own sisters and my temple, the Erechteum?"

"Your sisters are just fine. To protect them from industrial pollution and the effects of automobile exhaust, they have been moved inside the new Acropolis Museum. Exact replicas of all of you now support the Erechtheum portico, where you used to be. As for the Parthenon and the other temples, there is intensive work now under way to restore the damage sustained from wars, earthquakes, the weather elements, and also from earlier ill-conceived restoration efforts.

"Modern Greece, Karyatis, declared its independence from the Turks soon after you left. In the ensuing struggle the Acropolis being a Turkish fortress was besieged by Greek revolutionary forces and, unfortunately, some superficial damage was caused to the temples as a result of the war. On gaining its independence, one of the first acts of the new nation was to organize an Archaeological Service responsible for conserving and restoring the Acropolis. First priority was placed, of course, on the conservation and rebuilding of the

Parthenon. The many medieval buildings that cluttered the site were dismantled so that the necessary excavations, repair and restoration could be undertaken. A lot of good work has been done to date, but much still remains to be done.

XII

I DID NOT ASK TO BE RESCUED

So this is why I am here? In a strange land where I don't want to be, all because of a vain English nobleman anxious to impress his new bride? And, because of his paranoid chaplain who talked him into believing that I needed to be rescued?

Rescued from whom?

How absurd!

It must really have been painful for Sophia to go over this sad story with me, knowing all along that Edward, with whom she apparently is in a very close relationship, is partly responsible for my continued confinement here.

"But, Karyatis," I recall her saying, "Edward is merely one of several museum trustees," or words to that effect, as if wanting to absolve her friend of any direct responsibility on this matter. Even if he wanted to, Edward alone could not arrange for my freedom.

The only way for me to return home, she explained, is for

Parliament to enact the required legislation. The museum trustees cannot do it. They are prevented by statute from releasing any art object, unless a duplicate is already available in the collection which in my case of course there is none.

All that the museum trustees can do is to arrange for my return to the Acropolis on a temporary basis, -- in the form of a …loan.

As impatient as I am to return home, I find the thought of being "loaned" back to the Acropolis utterly preposterous. There will be no loan for me, thank you! When I return home it will be forever. If this requires an Act of the Parliament to accomplish, so be it.

No Parliament can deny me this right, especially in light of the circumstances that led to my being here. It is an issue of basic fairness. I was not created to be kept captive in a gloomy museum gallery in London. I belong outside, on my temple, under the bright Attica sun for all to admire.

But why would Parliament refuse my release, and in the process side with those responsible for masterminding this appalling theft? I know that theft is a harsh word, but how else can one describe the unauthorized removal from the Acropolis of crates full of some of the world's most unique and beautiful art?

The Elgin partisans will claim, as they have done so many times before, that a firman issued by the Ottoman authorities gave Elgin permission to remove the treasure. But, if the firman is such an important document for establishing the validity of their claim, why not produce it for all to see? According to Sophia, the original somehow no longer exists. It has been "lost" and only an Italian translation remains.

A translation made by whom? Lusieri, perhaps? Elgin's executioner on the Acropolis?

Is it possible -- please don't think that I am being paranoid now -- that a firman as such had never been issued by the Ottomans, and that its presumed existence is a mere fairy tale designed to cover up Elgin's mutilation of the Parthenon? There is nothing more absurd than the other defense being offered by the Elgin apologists, that by removing the Parthenon and other Acropolis sculptures Elgin actually helped "rescue" us.

I like to speak from personal experience.

For the record, I did not ask to be rescued!

Elgin rescued me, he claims, to prevent the Turks from crushing my form to produce mortar. How ludicrous! The Ottomans had been rulers of my hill for well over three hundred years, and not once during that entire period did I witness an instance of an Ottoman taking a statue down from its temple and crushing it for the purpose of producing mortar. Never! Why would they start doing so when Elgin appeared on the scene?

For well over two thousand years I stood my post on my temple, while legions of people of various faiths and nationalities -- Athenians, Macedonians, Romans, Goths, Byzantines, Franks and even Ottomans - came and left. Not once was I harmed, abused, or traumatized by any of them, not even during the times when armed men would confront each other in anger near where I was standing. Everyone it seemed, respected my presence and the sanctity of my temple.

Still, Elgin decided that I needed to be protected, that I needed rescuing?

"Remember me, Karyatis?" Sophia's familiar voice startles me.

"It's me, Sophia. I came to see you again," she adds, a lovely smile gracing her face. "I hope you haven't thought, that I have forgotten you."

"Of course not, Sophia. I figured that you were preoccupied with something very important. It's been several days, you know, since your last visit here."

"I know. I have been hard at work on your portrait."

"Will I get to see it?"

"Of course, as soon as I put the final touches on it. But I've come, Karyatis, for another reason. I have some news that you might be interested in hearing."

"News affecting me? What is it? Am I going home?"

"No! Not yet, I am afraid.

"I spent a lot of time pleading your case last week, both with people who want to keep you here and also others who agree that your place is back on the Acropolis. I also managed to draw Edward away from his duties long enough to hear his views on this matter. I thought, you'd want to hear what transpired."

It all began a few days ago, Karyatis, when one of London's more prestigious newspapers ran an article on what ostensibly was the British Museum's answer to press criticisms on the treatment of Greek students during their recent protest. But, instead of making his case and quitting, the author of the story decided to take on the entire issue of the Parthenon sculptures. What followed was a tirade of the worse kind, full of misinformation and half truths. It really sounded as if the man was bent on rewriting history.

Needless to say, I became quite furious, both at the author and the newspaper for publishing such rubbish.

The Greek students, he claimed, are supporting an untenable position by challenging the museum's legal ownership of the "Elgin marbles" and pressuring the trustees to return them to Greece. The museum trustees have no legal right to do so, even if they wanted to. The students had better cool it! The "Elgin marbles" are not going anywhere, not now, nor in the future. If Greece wishes to publicize her cultural heritage for the benefit of its many foreign visitors, the author continued, it should do so by exhibiting some of the art which it is now keeping in storage.

"The people of Britain," the article concluded, "are indebted to Lord Elgin for having rescued the Parthenon and other Acropolis sculptures from certain destruction, and for bringing them to our shores for all mankind to admire. Elgin has been unjustly defamed for far too long. It is time that he be recognized for what he truly was, a distinguished public servant who became aware of an acute need and decided to act upon it."

The cool and composed Sophia that you have gotten to know, Karyatis, over the past weeks can display a striking temper when provoked. The article's concluding paragraph did just that. It aroused my anger to no end.

Elgin is being unjustly defamed? He can't be serious, I shouted. Panting with anger, I reached for my laptop.

"Dear Editor," I typed hurriedly.

"How disappointing that the author of your article found it

necessary to rewrite history in an effort to convince your readers that the Parthenon sculptures should remain in the British Museum. In light of what actually happened, how can anyone seriously believe that Lord Elgin has been unjustly defamed, or that we the people of Britain are indebted to him for rescuing the Parthenon and other sculptures from the Acropolis.

"Elgin defamed himself by removing for personal reasons dozens of crates of some of the world's most beautiful and unique art, including ninety large pieces from the pediment, metopes, and frieze of the Parthenon.

"He had no permission from the people of Greece to do this, who after all are the owners of this art. They had no voice in the matter, being subjects of the Ottoman empire at that time. As for the Ottoman 'firman,' which Elgin's supporters claim as justification for his actions, it was by all accounts vague and only granted him permission to remove 'pieces of stone with inscriptions or figures.' I leave it to your readers to judge whether the sculptures that Elgin brought to our shores, and are now being exhibited in the Duveen Gallery at the British Museum, qualify as 'mere pieces of stone.'

"Rewriting history, as your article's author appears to be doing, can be extremely dangerous. Think of future generations being told, that the millions of black men, women, and children who were sold into slavery to Americans, were not really slaves, but had been brought to the United States as a humanitarian gesture to save them from their destitute home environment. And pity the millions, who might believe the tale."

Sincerely,
Sophia Parker, artist

"Sophia! What a great letter! You did it for me?"

"Yes. My regret is that I mailed it hurriedly, as it came out of my printer. I should have waited, toned it down a bit, especially that ill-tempered comment about the American slaves."

"Did you get any feed-back?"

"I sure did, from Edward of all people. How did I know that the paper would publish my letter on the very next day, and before I had a chance to tell him about it. He read it on his way to work. and it came as a real surprise to him."

On the morning that my letter appeared in the paper, Karyatis, I received several phone calls mostly from fellow artists. They were all highly complementary, as were many of the women in my morning exercise class. I was also pleased by two additional Letters to the Editor that appeared alongside mine.

"The British Museum has stalled long enough," noted the first writer. *"It is time to return the Parthenon sculptures where they belong. They are an integral part of the Parthenon and the greatest Hellenic cultural symbol. The sculptures represent the soul of Greece and provide a direct link to its past. I should know, for I am a Turk."*

Coming from a Turk, the support was especially gratifying. The Turks and Greeks, Karyatis, perhaps you don't know it, are not in the best of terms; it is all the result of centuries-old animosity between the two peoples.

The second letter, obviously prepared by someone much more knowledgeable with the issue, was in the form of an admonition to the Greek student protesters. *"This letter is being written by a Briton and a friend of your cause,"* opened the communication, *"but one, who is becoming increasingly concerned with the deteriorating state of the national debate on the Parthenon sculptures. Please resist the temptation to push us,"* he warned. *"If you wish the sculptures returned to the Acropolis you should appeal instead to our sense of fairness. We are age-old friends and admirers of your nation and have always done what is right by you. Many years ago we granted you the Ionian islands. In time, we will do the right thing also with the Parthenon sculptures.*

"Please keep in mind also, that many of our citizens think of the sculptures as being our own," he continued, *"so stop arguing the issue of ownership. Even the government of Greece is soft pedaling this aspect. It is not important who legally owns the sculptures; what is important is that they be returned to the Acropolis. There is precedent for repatriating art to the place of its origin. We did so recently in the case of art belonging to Burma and Scotland.*

"Construction of the new Museum in Athens," he concluded, *"coupled with a Greek Government expression of thanks to the British Museum for safekeeping the sculptures through the years, should go a long way toward resolving this issue."*

What a sensible man, I thought. Perhaps, appealing to the British sense of fair play is the way to go, rather than carrying on a protracted and useless argument with the British Museum, over who owns what and how the sculptures happened to have been acquired.

"Don't you agree, Karyatis?"

"I am sorry, Sophia, I really don't. I feel like the man from Turkey said in his letter. The British Museum has stalled long enough. Unless there is pressure brought upon it from the outside, it will not act. But please go on."

I have not had the opportunity yet, Karyatis, to visit the new Acropolis Museum, even though it's been open now for quite some time. So, I decided to inquire among my friends.

"You mean the one that was recently opened," asked Tom, a classmate of mine at Leeds University and a biologist by profession, with an enormous interest in the fine arts.

"Was there last summer. It is a building with a mission, built to accommodate under one roof all surviving Parthenon sculptures -- those held by Greece as well as those in the British Museum, if and when we decide to return them. It is truly a very beautiful structure, probably one of the most beautiful museums in Europe. The goal was to have it in place in time for the 2004 Summer Olympics held in Athens, but legal and other complications held up the work. It finally opened its doors in June 2009.

"The museum, Sophia, is located on a grassy slope on the foothills of the Acropolis, at a point less that half a mile away from the Parthenon. Its close proximity to the monument makes a strong argument that all Parthenon sculptures, being intrinsic parts of the temple, are meant to be viewed together and in their original setting, rather than in a chilly gallery two thousand miles away, as is the case with the marbles held in London.

"The centerpiece of the new museum is of course the Parthenon Gallery. Identical in size and orientation as the temple, it has on display only the Parthenon sculptures that Lord Elgin left behind, i.e. those that he decided not to remove. The sculptures that he did remove are depicted in the gallery by means of white casts. Casts of some of the sculptures held in the British Museum are also on display at the nearby Acropolis metro station. They too serve as reminders of Elgin's appalling act, and of the fact that nearly half of the Parthenon's carved decoration is still in London and not where it should be. ”

"Would you happen to know, Sophia, whether my sisters are already in the new museum?"

"They certainly are and according to photos that I have seen, there is space provided for you Karyatis at the precise location where you should be. Waiting for you to return."

"Very thoughtful of the museum people, but I am still here."

"Have patience, Karyatis. Millions worldwide feel strongly that the day when you will be returning home is fast approaching. There is great support in Britain and elsewhere for the return of the sculptures. There is also opposition, of course, from the British Museum. Would not the return of the marbles, it asks, set a precedent for other countries to come knocking at its door for their artifacts?

In a way, Karyatis, I can understand the museum's opposition. But what remains a true mystery to me, is why the British government is so strongly opposed to the restitution of the sculptures. Dozens of members of Parliament are in favor; every poll ever taken among the British public proves overwhelming support; opinion makers in the arts, the media, and the universities regularly speak out in favor of restitution. Still the British government is opposed. Greece has not made a convincing case, it claims, either “morally or culturally.”

Numerous persons outside the government, too, similarly

favor restitution and committees that support reunification operate in Britain and in sixteen other nations. The British committee has a long history of urging the common sense of keeping together all Acropolis art, rather than displaying some antiquities there and the remainder 2,000 miles away.

Needless to say, every one of your compatriots in Greece are feverishly working for your return, and so are millions of Hellenes in the Diaspora. A truly visionary lady, a world famous actress by the name of Melina Mercuri who later served as the Minister of Culture of Greece, was instrumental in organizing world public opinion in support of your cause. She addressed the people of Britain repeatedly on radio and television on the common sense of uniting in one location the masterpieces of the Acropolis, and brought also the same message to UNESCO, the United Nations organization concerned with cultural affairs. Sadly, Melina died before her work was finished, but a foundation named after her is keeping her vision alive. She will be there in spirit, Karyatis, when you return home.

Much of the international support for the return of the Parthenon marbles is due to her efforts. Greece's neighbor Turkey has also come out in favor of restitution. Turkey, says its government, considers it its responsibility to assist in this effort, since the seizure of the Acropolis art by Elgin took place during the period that Greece was occupied by the Ottomans.

"A lot of good, all this does to me, Sophia. I am still here, remember?"

"You must learn to be patient, Karyatis. Your day will come.

"Let me try to raise your spirits a bit, by recounting an amusing incident that occurred on the day that I visited Parliament to do a bit of lobbying on your behalf.

"Primarily because of your insistence, I no longer use the term 'Elgin marbles' when referring to the Acropolis antiquities, even though that term is used widely throughout Britain. The different designations are causing a lot of confusion with the general public, and even among some important persons who should know better.

"What?" asked one of our solons in utter surprise, when I suggested to him that the time had come for Britain to do what is right and return the Parthenon sculptures to Greece. "No way," he exploded. "If you give those bloody Greeks the Parthenon sculptures now, they'll be asking next for the Elgin marbles! No way. I would not give them either."

"That was very comical, Sophia!

"By the way, does Edward share this view?"

"Unfortunately, yes. He does know, of course, that both terms refer to the same art. But when it comes to you and the other Acropolis art being returned to Greece, he adheres strictly to the line of the British Museum. As a member of the museum trustees, it would be odd if he didn't."

On the day that I last talked to Edward on the issue of the Parthenon sculptures, he had come out of a meeting of the museum trustees. He looked tired and was pressed for time, still it had been two days since my Letter to the Editor had appeared in the paper and he seemed anxious to discuss it.

"What was that all about, Sophia," he asked while reaching into his packet for the newspaper clippings on the original article and its three responses. "I never knew that you have such strong views on this matter. And, why did you have to accuse the author of the article of rewriting history? Frankly, I don't believe that he did.

"Regardless of what others may have told you, Lord Elgin had the approval of the Ottoman authorities for removing from the ruins of the Parthenon the architectural sculptures that he did. When he arrived on the scene, the various temples on the Acropolis and especially the Parthenon were in a sorry state. By removing this art and bringing it to London, where over the past two hundred years it has been displayed for all to admire, Elgin not only rescued it from ruin, but helped preserve it for future generations.

"In your letter, Sophia, you didn't come outright for the return of the Elgin collection to Greece, but from your language it appears that this had been your intent. But I thought you knew. We, at the museum, are prohibited by law from permanently disposing any objects other than duplicates. Returning the Parthenon treasures, which incidentally are among the best loved of all the museum holdings, would be a betrayal of our trust. It would also establish an awful precedent, which could result in time in the piecemeal dismemberment of the British Museum as we know it today."

"To the people of Greece, Edward," I responded softly, "the Parthenon is not merely a beautiful temple that needs to be preserved whole. It is a lot more than that! It is that nation's Crown Jewels, America's Liberty Bell, France's Arch de Triumph, all in one. How would we feel, if because of a past international misfortune, Nelson's column had ended up in Paris and the French refused to return it?

"As for the argument that the return of the Parthenon sculptures would lead to requests for the return of other Greek art in British museums, it simply does not hold. Greece is not asking for the return of any other art, only that which was originally part of the Parthenon, their nation's greatest national symbol, and as you know, one of the outstanding monuments of humanity. The Parthenon exemplifies Greece's contributions to the cultural heritage of all mankind, and as such, the monument should be reunified and its integrity restored.

"Julie Ainsworth, at whose gallery I have displayed some of my work in the past, and with whom I've discussed this matter has a good idea, I think. Forget about the matter of who owns the Elgin collection, she says. What difference does it make today whether Elgin was a saint or a sinner? What is needed is a kind of accommodation which would be acceptable to both nations; a shared ownership of the collection perhaps, or loaning the collection to Greece on an indefinite basis in exchange for some recent Greek archaeological finds."

"I don't believe that the museum would be interested in any such arrangement, Sophia," he answered curtly. "The Elgin marbles have a permanent home, and that is in the British Museum."

"But, why Edward? Why are you so intent on supporting the museum's hard line?" I recall asking him, my voice suggesting annoyance at his last comment. "The people of Greece can certainly preserve and display the sculptures with as much care as we do."

Our views were clearly diametrically opposed, Karyatis. It made no sense continuing the discussion, with Edward repeatedly sounding as hard as he did, when the subject had first come up. "The marbles are here to stay, Sophia," he repeated. "I am afraid this is closed case."

Keep it civil, keep it rational, Sophia, I reminded myself. You don't want this to escalate into open warfare!

"I am disappointed, young lady. Somehow, I had hoped that Edward because of his association with you, would turn out to be a friend and supporter."

"I am disappointed, too, Karyatis. But the more I listen to his views, the more convinced I become of his sincerity on this issue. He's not merely mouthing the museum's line; he truly believes in what he's saying."

Edward came by my studio later that evening, and again the issue of the Parthenon sculptures came up. Unlike Julie's suggestion, he reported, supporters of restitution are planning an action in the courts to establish the legal ownership of the marbles. They are basing their argument on an old legal principle, that one cannot transfer title of something not legally his own. And since, according to their view, Lord Elgin never had title to the marbles ("having stolen them"), he could not transfer them legally to the British government and in turn to the museum. Several persons behind this action are even suggesting that because the "theft" occurred in Greece, Greek law should prevail in making the final determination on this issue.

"I can see where one could make a good argument, Edward, that title to the sculptures was and still rests with the people of Greece," I recall telling him.

"Only if you ignore the fact, Sophia," he interrupted, "that

Elgin had the permission of the Ottoman authorities to remove the art. I am aware of the arguments that perhaps he exceeded the terms of his firman, but the fact that he did have authority to remove art is indisputable.

"Then, too Sophia, everyone seems to focus on Elgin's original firman. But, there was a second one you know, which was secured later for him by Sir Robert Adair his replacement as Ambassador to Constantinople . The second firman instructed the Ottoman authorities in Athens to allow the embarkation of the antiquities collected by Elgin, which were languishing then in a warehouse in Piraeus. If the Ottoman authorities believed, as some people do now that Elgin had "stolen" the marbles, they would not have given permission for them to be loaded on a ship for their trip to England.

"Elgin's critics also ignore the fact, that a lot of material from the Parthenon had been removed even before Elgin arrived on the scene. The British Museum holds many pieces of course, but Parthenon remains can also be found at the Louvre in Paris, and also in the museums of the Vatican, Vienna, Munich, and Copenhagen. As for the alleged damage to the temple during Elgin's operations, the critics again are not familiar with all the facts. By far the biggest damage to the Parthenon occurred when the old temple was converted into a Christian Church. Large sections of the temple were removed to make room for the apse, most metopes were deliberately defaced, and numerous statues were intentionally damaged as idols to pagan gods. Compared to the harm caused in the name of Christianity, Elgin's agents were responsible only for minimal damage to the temple."

The more I listened to Edward, Karyatis, the more convinced I became that he was adamant in his beliefs. The fear continues to persist, he added, among the majority of the museum trustees, that sending the Parthenon art back to Greece will establish a very bad precedent by opening the floodgates for similar requests from other nations -- a true Pandora's box. There would be no end to the claims for restitution, not only on the British Museum but on all great museums of the world. Egypt wants the Rosetta Stone returned to Cairo, and also Cleopatra's Needle which now stands on the Embankment. Nigeria is asking for the repatriation of the Benin bronzes, and Ethiopia is pressing for the return of numerous early Christian relics.

"Are we, and the other large museums in the west, expected to empty our galleries and return the various artifacts that we are holding to the nations of their origin? Should the Mona Lisa be returned to Italy? It does sound kind of foolish, doesn't it. Museums in the west are full of art which originated in other nations. Through history, victors in war have plundered the antiquities and works of art of their vanquished foes. The looting of treasures has been going on since Biblical times.

"As for the Parthenon marbles, even if they were to be returned to Greece, they would not be placed back on the temple itself, but simply be exhibited in another museum. The art would be transported from one museum to another."

"That's it?"

"I am afraid so."

"Yet, you keep telling me Sophia that the day of my return home is fast approaching? But, everything that I have heard since, seems to support the opposite. Listening to Edward especially, it all sounds pretty gloomy."

"Have faith Karyatis. All that is required for you to gain your freedom is a political decision. The Greek government has made concessions. Who owns the sculptures, it says, is no longer relevant; what matters is where they should be. All it wants is for the Parthenon to be reunified, to bring together all its pieces in one place, and to have its integrity restored.

"In time our government will do the right thing, Karyatis. In my heart, I know that it will. Please believe me, and when the day of your freedom comes, I'll be there waiting for you at the airport in Athens!"

"I certainly hope so, Sophia.

"Incidentally, where are you heading to now?"

"A holiday, as soon as I am done with your portrait. A symposium on Byzantine art is scheduled in Thessaloniki later this month and I am anxious to attend. Unfortunately, Edward will not be joining me. He has too many work commitments here in London."

"Oh please take me along, Sophia! Please!"

"You know that I cannot.

"You've got to be patient, my Hellenic friend. Be patient, just a bit longer? Please!

"Your day will come, believe me! Our government will do the right thing, and you will be on your way home, where you long to be."

CHRONOLOGY

BC

447-438	Construction of the Parthenon
431-404	War between Athens and Sparta
429	Death of Pericles
356	Philip II of Macedonia launches his conquest of Hellas
336	Philip II is assassinated
336-323	Alexander the Great expands his empire into Africa and Asia
323	Death of Alexander
323-276	Alexander's successors carve up his empire
146	Hellas becomes a Roman province
87	Sulla sacks Athens after a long siege

AD

50	Saint Paul introduces Christianity to Athenians
267	Goths invade Hellas; ravage Athens
311	Emperor Constantine recognizes Christianity
395	Visigoths enter Athens
529	Emperor Justinian orders the closing of the Athenian academies
723-843	Iconoclast dispute rocks Byzantium
1054	Great Schism between Orthodox East and Rome
1204	Crusaders sack Constantinople

1205-1455	Franks, Catalans, and Florentines rule Athens
1456	Ottomans occupy Athens and rule until 1833
1687	Parthenon damaged severely by Morosini
1799	Lord Elgin appointed British Ambassador to the Ottoman Government
1802	The Karyatis is forcibly removed from her temple and transported to London

SELECTED TERMS

Agora : market place and center of political activity in a city.

Cella : enclosed inner room in a temple; sanctuary of a deity.

Chiton : full-length item of clothing

Chlamys : cloak worn by men, usually fastened on shoulder.

City-State : usually a city and its surrounding area.

Ecclesia : an assembly of people; also a Christian church.

Firman : a permit issued by an Ottoman authority.

Himation : cloak or wrap worn by both men and women.

Hoplite : heavily armed Greek warrior.

Metope : square panel in an Doric frieze, plain or sculptured.

Peplos : sleeveless, loose fitting garment worn by women.

Stoa : elongated building used as a meeting place.

Stratigos : the executive of a city-state; military commander

Trireme: large ship, usually warship, with three banks of oars.

Made in the USA
Charleston, SC
06 August 2013